The Dance Centre Presents

GISELLE

CHI VARNADO

GnomeWood Press
P.O. Box 404
Ramona, CA 92065
GnomeWoodPress.com

Cover illustration by Pam Wilder
Book cover and interior design by Monkey C Media
Edited by Adrianne Moch

First Edition
Printed in the United States of America

ISBN: 978-1-7341423-0-3 (Trade Paperback)
ISBN: 978-1-7341423-1-0 (E-Pub)

Library of Congress Control Number: 2019920282

For all who dream of dancing:

Life is a dance—
part choreography, part freestyle.

Giselle

The Romantic ballet, Giselle, was composed by Adolphe Adam and first performed in Paris in 1841. In this tragic story, a lovely young peasant girl falls for the disguised nobleman, Albrecht. When she discovers the truth, she dies of a broken heart and he has to face the other-worldly consequences of his dishonest actions.

DANCESPIRATION

Dance can be what literally saves us.

Sometimes a kid can feel like they're going to jump out of their own skin if they have to stay stationary very long. I, for one, was one of those. Almost constant motion was my motto: running, jumping, riding a bicycle, shooting baskets or playing tetherball by myself, bouncing to musical rhythms… I was fortunate that both my mom and grandmother recognized this and enrolled me in ballet at a young age. In this way, my need for physical activity, a love of classical music, and the passion to express myself theatrically could all be addressed. Plus, I loved the hard work and discipline that ballet required. Even later, as a dance major in college, I viewed my morning ballet class as dance therapy. It's what I looked forward to. Dance is hard work, but it's also play. Let's celebrate both and enjoy the fusion that this art form provides!

—Love,
Miss Chi

"Young readers will love this story, which allows a glimpse inside the lives of dancers at a small ballet studio. A must read for aspiring dancers and for anyone intrigued by the world of ballet."
—T. Greenwood, author of
Keeping Lucy and *Rust & Stardust*

"Giselle is so relatable! As a former student of ballet and a current teacher of middle school dancers, it was easy to imagine my students as the characters in the story. Chi Varnado's writing makes you care about each character and their journey as a young dancer. What a fun and positive story for young readers and lovers of ballet. And I love the use of ballet terminology in italics, almost like the words are dancing on the page!"
—Erica Buechner,
professional dancer/choreographer

"*Giselle* is an enticing read, filled with complex characters and interesting plot lines. The story circles around a group of teenage girls and a few boys involved in a dance production. As with teenage characters the story is dramatic as it delves into their interpersonal relationships, but there are light moments too. The characters are likeable and diverse. It also dips into important teenage issues like pregnancy and anorexia. A good book to read with your teen to facilitate those discussions that might be difficult to initiate. As a reader I enjoyed the book and would like to see further development of these characters beyond their introduction in this story."
—Cindy Z, K-12 School Library Technician

"***The Dance Center Presents Giselle*** is a discerning glimpse into the life, passion, and anxieties of your local youth dance company. For those who dance, Giselle delves into a world so familiar. Readers will find themselves and those around them mirrored in the real-to-life characters in this story. For those who now only dance when dreaming, Giselle is a fond trip down memory lane, with many pleasant and reminiscent detours. And for those who have never danced, Giselle will introduce you into the wonderful, and often emotional, world of dance. Varnado has fashioned a masterful work developing genuine characters struggling through issues so close to any reader's heart. Giselle is the perfect book for a young child who is curious about dance, for the dancing youth living through all these same experiences, and for the adult who once lived that dance life or who ever wondered about the dancers' world."

—Dr. James Gaskin, PhD; Professor of Information
Systems; Marriott School of Business; Brigham
Young University; Former Dancer and Gymnast

Contents

1

WINTER SESSION BEGINS

Randi

Be gracious. After all—we get to dance!

Randi twirls effortlessly in an outside *pirouette*—single, double, triple—spotting the bright-blue stage light. Her balance remains perfect even though her *tours* slow down and eventually stop. She remains *en pointe*, holding her position on the tiptoes of a single foot, and the crowd goes wild for her eleven consecutive turns. Adrenaline surges while she retains perfect balance.

When the bell rings, she nearly catapults off her chair, as she snaps out of the daydream she's been having.

It's probably from watching that old dance video, White Nights, where the ballet dancer, Baryshnikov, performs eleven tours in a row. Unbelievable!

Randi smiles at her friend, Paige, and shoves her algebra book and papers into her backpack. Today is the first day back at the Dance Centre after winter break, and she's ready to jump out of her skin in anticipation.

"I'm so out of shape I can hardly wait to get back. Come on, Paige! My mom's probably here by now waiting for us."

"I'm coming already," Paige says, tucking her unruly, dishwater-blonde hair behind her ears.

"I'm stoked that ballet is starting back today, aren't you?"

"Of course. It feels like winter break's been longer than two weeks."

"Oh, yeah, my leg muscles are definitely weaker." Randi misses the feel of her body in peak condition, strong and reliable.

The girls run to their lockers, grab their ballet totes, and race out to the front of the school where Randi's mom is waiting in the crowded lot.

"I brought you girls a snack. I hope you like peanut butter and celery, Paige."

"Thanks. I'll need all the energy I can get to keep up with Randi. She's so good."

"I'm glad I finally convinced you to join ballet," Randi says. "What was it, like, three years ago?"

"Technically, three-and-a-half, now that it's mid-year," Paige says as she pulls a sticky, brown-covered stalk out of her baggie.

Randi can't wait to get back to ballet. When she's not dancing, she's daydreaming about it, watching dance videos, or scouring the latest *Pointe Magazine*. She bounces in her seat as they drive the back way across town to avoid most of the after school traffic. When they arrive at the Dance Centre parking lot, Randi bolts out of the car.

"Thanks, Mom!" she yells, while Paige remains, licking peanut butter from her fingers.

Randi pushes open the glass door and drops her dance bag under the front window. A familiar Mozart concerto is playing. Randi turns to glance at her reflection in the floor-to-ceiling mirrors that cover the entire front wall and *chassés* over to Miss Val, who is going over some notes. The teacher looks up, smiles, and reaches out to give Randi a welcoming hug.

"It sure feels good to be back." Randi revels in the readiness that her body feels in anticipation of the ballet exercises that give her such pleasure. She itches to begin the *barre*.

"It's been a while, huh?" The tall, slender woman radiates elegance. "I was wondering. Could you stay after class a few minutes? I'd like to talk to you about something."

"Sure," Randi says, as her palms start to sweat. *What could it be about?* A faint, sharp odor fills her nostrils, and she notices a fresh gleam on the wood floor.

Paige opens the door, sending a shaft of reflected sunlight into the room. Miss Val walks toward the desk, her lithe body graceful and confident.

What on earth could Miss Val want to talk to me about? I rack my brain for an explanation, but find none. Does she want to demote me to the Intermediate class? Please no!

I've worked so hard on my pointe technique. I'm one of the best dancers here—besides Bree, of course.

Bree is a senior, and has danced with Miss Val forever.

I don't want to leave, but what about that other dance studio in town? No, too much drama there. At least that's what everyone says. Besides, I've been here six amazing years, and they're like my family. It feels like home.

Other familiar faces enter the studio, and Miss Val sits down at the desk, where she takes tuition payments and fills out registration forms.

At last, class begins.

"*Demi* and straight, *elevé* and lower, *grand plié* with a simple *port-de-bras*." Miss Val demonstrates with a graceful arm, resting her other hand on the *barre*. "After a balance in *soussus*, then turn around and begin the other side. We have a lot of catch-up work to do after being off for the break."

Randi feels the usual wave of transcendence envelop her when the beautiful music begins. With the specific use of her muscles, her body eases into her other self—the person she becomes when she dances. In the *cambré* back, she is almost one with the music and the movement. It's a combination that transports her away from her usual worries about homework, tests and other unpleasant concerns. *This* is why she dances. She is in love with who she becomes.

"Randi, pick up your ankles. You know better than that." Miss Val is always getting on her about rolling in.

Randi tenses. During the next *plié*, she concentrates on her knees lining up over her toes, as if a plumb line hangs from them. She carefully tries to work with the proper amount of turnout for her body, to prevent injury.

Thank goodness I can do it better than most of the other girls. It's partly genetic, but mostly training. Turnout is hard work.

The intense focus and concentration are already causing moisture to trickle down her spine.

"That's better," says Miss Val.

After the last exercise, the students carry the portable *barres* to the wall before stretching in the center. Randi joins the others on the floor. They all usually bend over their straightened legs or sit in the splits, while Miss Val marks the pattern in the corner. But this time, the instructor sits on the newly varnished floor with them, apologizing for the smell of paint, and welcomes the class back.

"So, what ballet are we going to do this year?" Randi asks. She knows she isn't the only one dying to find out.

"Do you know yet?" Deanne asks.

Randi still doesn't think she's ever seen anyone with hair as bright red as that girl's. Deanne and Miss Val's oldest daughter, Brindle, are just eighth graders. Their petite, Hispanic friend Sophia is the youngest in class and a year behind them in school.

Randi notices how much they've improved since last semester—especially Deanne. Annie, who's older than the others and attends the local community college part time, is even thinner than she was before. Randi wishes she was that skinny, but she accepts that she doesn't have the same body type.

"Well," Miss Val begins. "Most likely, *Giselle*. It's my favorite ballet of all time."

"How about *Snow White*?"

"What's that smell, Sophia?" Deanne interjects, making a sudden face. "B.O.?"

"Welcome back, Deanne," Randi says. "Did you forget how hard we work in here? It's only been two weeks."

"It's not all glamour, you know," Paige teases.

"Hey, I know. Let's do *Toy Story*," Sophia says, as she reaches up to fix her long, black braid.

The girls erupt in laughter.

"You would want to do that. You're such a child," Deanne says.

That was a little juvenile, even if it was meant as a joke.

"Now, now," Miss Val interrupts. "Let's be nice."

"When can we start rehearsing?" Randi asks.

"Probably next month. But for now, using all the time we can to work on technique is essential. *Before* we start rehearsing!" She shakes her head and continues. "If we can't execute ballet steps with confidence, we certainly won't be able to beautifully perform the roles required in a story ballet, now will we?"

"No," Randi answers. "Hey, where's Bree? Has anyone seen her lately?"

Miss Val scans the room and speaks hesitantly. "Bree won't be coming back this year so you'll all have to step it up a bit."

What?

The class starts firing questions about Bree's whereabouts, but Miss Val deflects them.

Why? What happened?

"Okay. Time's a-wasting. Let's dance. Oh, I almost forgot. Here's your new dancespiration. *Be gracious. After all—we get to dance!*" she says, sharing yet another of her fun little quips with the students.

Miss Val smiles, claps her hands, and begins demonstrating the center pattern they are to execute, which includes *pas de basques* and waltz turns.

Randi has a hard time concentrating.

What does Miss Val want to talk to me about?

She shakes her thoughts away to focus on the task at hand—dance—and picks herself up off the floor to start marking through the steps Miss Val shows them.

She walks through the steps, in miniature, which helps her memorize them. The slow *adagio* gives her ample opportunity to express herself. Randi stretches her torso upward as she sinks into *plié* and opens her arms in *port-de-bras*. A traveling pattern across the floor follows, linking *faillis*, *assemblés*, and *tour jetés*. The turn combination makes her dizzy, and she veers off course.

"Focus on your spotting, dear," Miss Val says.

The dancers repeat the pattern, but Randi keeps falling out of the *arabesque* turn.

Why is this so hard? Just last month I nailed it.

Miss Val interjects, "You're going up in *relevé* too soon in the turn, Randi. Pay attention to the *plié* and your spot, and your body will sense when to rise."

Randi tries it when she starts across the other diagonal, but can't make it work.

Deanne continues past her, seemingly unfazed by the sequence.

"It's easy for me," she says when Randi catches up.

"I guess I'm out of practice," Randi says, breathing hard.

"You know, I took a couple of master classes during the break so I could maybe get a solo role this year," Deanne says dismissively.

Jeez.

The *révérence*, at the end, brings composure and calm to Randi's sweaty body and before she knows it, class is over. But she feels like a failure. She'd expected to do so much better than she did today. She should have practiced more over the break.

The dancers sit on the floor by the door, taking off their *pointe* shoes, and putting on street shoes and clothes. Randi watches Annie drift, waif-like, out the front door like an elegant skeleton. It's finished too soon, and now Miss Val motions for her to go to the other side of the studio, away from the others.

As her fellow dancers leave, Randi's heart thumps hard. Sweat doesn't trickle, but cascades down the center of her back.

What have I done wrong? Did I do something bad without even knowing it? Why else would I be singled out?

Her stomach is in knots, but she smiles and waves goodbye to Paige, trying to appear nonchalant.

After an excruciating three minutes while Miss Val seems to be taking her time, marking role cards at the desk, Randi's heart is ready to explode in her chest.

Let's get this over with—whatever it is. She pleads with her eyes, but Miss Val never looks up.

She knows she could've danced better today, but her body just wouldn't cooperate.

Miss Val made me nervous because she said she wanted to talk. It can't be because I'm not very talented—can it?

"Sorry about the wait," Miss Val finally says, striding over to the corner where Randi stands.

She tries to take a deep breath, to brace herself for what might follow. But the air, enough of it anyway, won't flow in. She's left with shallow inhales. Trying to appear calm, she manages a grin.

"You've improved a lot lately," her teacher begins.

Here it comes. The room darkens when a cloud covers the sun.

Miss Val looks directly at her. "How would *you* like to dance the lead this year?"

What? Did I hear right? Randi's jaw drops, and she finds herself unable to form any words.

"Bree isn't available, and you happen to be next in line. It's a big step, I know, but I think you can handle it."

Randi looks around the room and wiggles her fingers, to make sure she's not dreaming, and squeaks out, "But I didn't do very well today."

Miss Val waves at the two Beginning students coming in. "It's one day, Randi. Don't be so hard on yourself. I have faith in you. You'll have to work hard, no doubt. But I'll help you. Okay?"

Randi nods, uncertainly, and a smile forms. "Wow. Thank you." Her feet are glued to the floor as Miss Val walks across the room to greet the next class.

Is this really happening? To me?

She pictures herself dancing a solo on the big stage— leaping through the air and turning *pirouettes*, with the audience applauding enthusiastically. But then the image vanishes, and sheer terror replaces it. She's not nearly as good a dancer as Bree, and her technique is sorely lacking.

What's Miss Val thinking? There's no way I can pull this off—at least not this year. Or can I?

2

A Surprise Landing

Randi

When stretching, breathe deeply;
your muscles will thank you.

Morning sunlight streams into the bright yellow kitchen and Randi yawns. Her older brother, David, is standing in front of the refrigerator with the door wide open. He chugs milk straight from the container.

"That's disgusting! You can't drink out of the carton like that!" Randi yells, as she reaches for the bagels in the cupboard. She's not a germaphobe, but that's gross.

"Oh, yes, I can. I just did. The problem with you is that you never learned the difference between *can* and *may*," he says, turning back and taking another swallow.

Sometimes I wonder how we can possibly be related.

His sandy blond hair, which now hangs over his ears, contrasts sharply with her dark brown ponytail.

Plus, he's thrilled to chase a stupid ball around the soccer field, like a mad dog.

He's so annoying.

Mom walks into the kitchen carrying a load of laundry. "Can't you two ever lay off each other? All you do is bicker." She sets the basket on the island and tightens her bathrobe sash.

"She thinks she owns the world now that she gets to be Giselle." He mocks the word *Giselle* with feigned importance and then replaces the milk back on the top shelf of the refrigerator and closes the stainless steel door.

"Nu-huh. That's not true," Randi says, waving a knife above her bagel. "I was shocked to get it, I'll have you know." *Just how many days are there until he goes off to college?*

She drops the knife into the sink, causing a sharp clatter, and glares at him. Dancing the lead role this year makes her anxious enough, and his belittling doesn't help her already frayed nerves. Ever since Miss Val had pulled her aside to tell her the shocking news, she's been both excited and absolutely terrified.

David rolls his eyes and starts to leave the room. Mom catches his elbow. "Don't pick on your sister. You know she's worked very hard for this, don't you? And she's right. She didn't know that the lead role would land in her lap this way. But it did. And by the way, you seem to be getting some pretty lucky breaks yourself, Mister. You're a good soccer player, but sometimes we end up in the right place at the right time. Don't you think?"

Mom's always so diplomatic.

He scratches his messy head absentmindedly. "Well." He pauses. "Sure. I guess so. I didn't think I'd ever get to play forward."

Randi watches her brother, who isn't usually this reflective or pleasant, take the heavy basket and carry it to the washer for Mom.

Oh yeah. There was something about when the team was short on players, and he'd gotten to move up that day, getting to play offense instead of defense. That was a lucky break for him.

"We gotta go to school. Are you ready, Randi?" David grabs the keys from the peg and heads toward the door.

"Fine." *He's so irritating.* "Bye, Mom," she says and follows him out to the car.

Why does he have to make things even harder than they already are? He has no clue what I'm up against. I know I'm not ready to dance well enough to make that starring role shine, like Bree always did. And we still haven't found out what happened to her. She isn't even in school. Did she move away?

That evening, Randi is still rattled by the nagging image of blowing it as Giselle and letting everyone down, so she calls her grandma in Hawaii. She hasn't seen her in six months, but it feels like a year.

"How are you my little coyote?" This was the pet name she'd given Randi when she was little and too shy to look people in the eye.

"I'm fine. And you? How are the cats?" Randi loves hearing about Nana's kitties, but she can't wait to tell her the big news so she interrupts her answer. "Guess what, Nana? I got the lead role in our ballet, *Giselle*! Can you believe it?"

"That's wonderful, sweetheart. How exciting!"

"I know. I can hardly believe that Miss Val chose me!" She takes a few deep breaths and reminds herself that Miss Val told her to have faith. *Boy, I'm really going to have to psych myself up for this. Think positive and work hard.*

"Oh, I can understand why she did. You're a beautiful dancer, Randi."

Her head swims with the image of dancing on stage as the prima ballerina and she tells Nana that she's taking Bree's place. "But we don't even know where she went! And there's not even going to be an understudy, at least that I know of."

"Wow, girl, you've got your work cut out for you then, huh? Miss Val must really believe in you." Her grandma knows about the core group of the Advanced ballet class since Randi goes on about them every time they talk on the phone. But then Randi remembers her manners.

"Oh yeah—and how are your pretty kitties?"

Nana has a group of feral cats that congregate on her back stoop every evening, anticipating their usual scraps and leftovers. Randi knows this from visiting her every summer.

"They're all still here and kicking. Oh, and Randi, you should've seen the rooster that barged into the middle of them tonight. Those poor kitties didn't know what to make of him. They just tore out of there."

"The cats were afraid of a chicken?"

"I think he just took them by surprise."

Randi's nervous thoughts return. "Interesting. Hey, Nana? I'm kind of scared I won't be able to perform as Giselle very well. I'm nowhere near as good as Bree was, and I feel like I don't know what I'm doing at all sometimes."

"I'm sure you'll do just fine. Don't worry so much."

"But there's this Deanne girl who's trying to show me up. She acts like she likes me one minute and the next she's snotty. And she's always sucking up to Miss Val."

"Now, Randi. You listen to me. You are a beautiful dancer and I know you can do it. Your mother used to worry about not being good enough for college. But she was. She even made it onto the Dean's List. I wish she hadn't dropped out before getting a bachelor's degree, but that was her choice. She really lacked confidence back then. *You* have an opportunity right now, my dear. You can do absolutely whatever it is you set your mind to. It's your decision."

By the time Randi hangs up the phone, the majority of her self-doubt has dissipated. *Too bad it won't last. Maybe if I could feel this way often enough then I'd be a better dancer.*

Randi's thrilled when February finally arrives, and they begin rehearsing their parts and dances for *Giselle*. Every year, Miss Val evaluates the capabilities of each

Advanced dancer and takes into consideration how many students there are to determine which ballets are possible. It's fun how she incorporates all the dance forms into the story: ballet, modern, hip hop, tumbling, and more. Randi doesn't know of any other studio that does this.

On this particular afternoon, they're going to start learning one of the group pieces, since the Advanced students are all in class together on Tuesdays. After a short *barre*, Miss Val sits down with them while they stretch. She begins to tell them the story of *Giselle*. Randi sits in her right splits and watches sunlight from the big windows dance off the mirrors and project onto the curtain pulled across the back of the room. As she leans over her front leg, she concentrates on Miss Val's dancespiration, takes a deep breath, and relaxes down farther.

"Well, this tale is bittersweet and heart-wrenching, like so many ballets. Giselle falls in love with Albrecht, a duke disguised as a peasant. He, however, is engaged to a noblewoman who he does not love. Giselle eventually learns the truth and dies of a broken heart."

Even though I already know what the ballet is about, I love listening to Miss Val tell the story.

"She becomes a Wili, to join the ghosts who seek nighttime revenge on unsuspecting men. Hilarion is also a peasant, like her, and seeks her affections. In our rendition, Hilarion visits Giselle's grave where he is forced to dance to his death by the sister Wilis. Albrecht nearly suffers the same fate, but is finally spared by the magic of Giselle's love for him."

Paige sits up straight and in a hoity toity voice says, "Another fable about the stupidity of men?" and everyone cracks up. "I don't know, but isn't it funny how most of the men in these story ballets are completely at the mercy of the women?" She looks around at the group and smiles engagingly through her slightly crooked front teeth.

"They are, huh," says Brindle, grinning at Deanne and Sophia.

I watch Paige out of the corner of my eye. How does she always seem so relaxed? And then, Deanne gives me an evil glare.

"But we don't have any guys," Annie says. Her cropped black hair frames her cute little face perfectly. She looks like a movie star and actually does get some small modeling jobs. Maybe being half-Chinese is what makes her pretty and exotic.

Miss Val breaks in, putting her hands up. "I talked with the high school dance department and there are two boys interested in joining us. They should be here next week."

Of course, it's difficult to rope many boys into ballet, especially in a small town like Nuevo, even though it's only an hour away from the big city of San Diego. But Miss Val always seems to get what's required for these story ballets. Randi walks her hands forward on the wood floor into a "pancake" from her straddle.

"Who are they?" Deanne asks, brushing a bright red curl behind her ear.

"Their names are Jack, who will play Albrecht, and Todd, who will be Hilarion."

"I know them," Randi says, straightening up quickly. "Jack's kind of cute, too." She giggles along with the class, but her face is heating up and she's sure it must be beet red. "And he can actually dance." *Perhaps that sounds more objective.* He's in her dance production class at school.

Miss Val announces what parts each of them will be playing. "Obviously, you can't all be cast in lead roles. You'll have to be good sports."

And they are, for the most part. But Randi, and probably the others, too, still wonders what happened to Bree. After all, she had been destined for the lead role again this year.

"Randi is going to play Giselle. Annie will be Giselle's mother in Act One and the Queen Wili, Myrthe, in Act Two. The noblewoman who is betrothed to Albrecht will be Paige. Everyone else will be peasants in Act One and Wilis in Act Two, getting to dance the poor fellows into a tizzy. Paige, you'll also be a Wili in Act Two. Your group will lead the Intermediate ballet since they are also Wilis." Miss Val looks around at them to make sure they understand.

"Who are the Beginners going to be?" Randi asks, remembering how all the students at the studio are included in these story ballets.

Deanne is staring at her again.

What the heck?

"They will be villagers," Miss Val answers. "We need more of them for Act One."

She still can't believe that she actually gets to dance the lead role this year, and can't figure out why Deanne keeps looking at her like that.

"Okay, everybody. Up and at 'em! Let's learn the dance of the Wilis."

Miss Val places everyone in their positions and explains to begin slow and enticingly and then speed up into a frenzy. Randi and her ghostly sisters will swirl, circle, and dance the poor helpless fellows toward their demise. "Lots of *chaînes*, *jeté entournants* and *fouetté* turns," explains their fearless leader.

Randi can't help but notice Deanne picking up the dance sequences more quickly than she is. In one pass across the diagonal, she overtakes her in long-strided *piqué* turns, and almost collides with her.

Doesn't she know that I'm supposed to stay in front?

Miss Val calls out, "Step out more, Randi! Reach for those *piqué* turns!"

I'm trying, but it's difficult when Deanne is breathing down my neck and passing me by.

During the next segment, the dreaded *fouetté* turns actually go better than expected and Randi nails the ending in a lunge.

"Good job, Randi. And Deanne! Much improved!" Miss Val shouts.

Great. She's good at those, too.

3

Oh, The Life of a Wili

Deanne

*Take a breath, or three, and
let go of those worries.*

Deanne lies on top of her bed immersed in the latest novel that her best friend, Miss Val's oldest daughter, Brindle, had recommended. She likes books, of course, but it's difficult to keep up with that girl's voracious reading appetite. Her latest binge consists of novels about dragons and medieval historical fiction. Deanne tries to match her pace, finding the subjects fascinating and fun to talk about with Brindle.

Is this what having a sister of my own might be like?

Growing up as an only child with two parents who have full-time careers gives her lots of time to be alone and daydream—except for the hours she spends at the dance studio, in school, or attending church activities. And once in a while, she still fiddles around with the recorder she learned to play in elementary school.

"Hi, Deanne, I'm home." She hears her mother call from downstairs.

She hadn't realized how late it is already. A good book can do that, she muses.

"Could you come down and set the table please? Your father will be home any minute."

Deanne closes her book, carefully replacing the marker, and goes downstairs to help get dinner ready.

Her mother takes the lid off the crock pot and sniffs at the chicken and potatoes.

"How was your day, dear? Did you finish your homework? Oh, and don't forget, there's youth group tonight."

Mother has a way of spraying out questions and reminders, like fragments of a shotgun shell, not waiting to hear answers before starting again. And how could I possibly forget? I've been going every Wednesday evening for as long as I can remember.

They play Bible verse games, put on plays, and socialize with other Christian kids in the community. She usually looks forward to it, and even if she's tired or has too much homework and doesn't really feel like going, she's generally glad she went.

Deanne opens the buffet drawer and pulls out three white cloth napkins. She arranges them at each side of the formal table and one at the head, for Father.

"Yes, Mother. I finished my homework and I haven't forgotten about youth group. Could we stop and pick up Brindle tonight? I think I've finally convinced her to come check it out." *I sure hope she likes it.*

"That's wonderful, honey."

Right on time, her father walks into the kitchen and gives each of them his usual peck on the cheek. After they're seated at the table, he says grace and then picks up the platter and dishes a chicken leg and a few small potatoes onto his plate before passing it to Deanne. Mother hands her a helping of crisp, green salad and pours ice water from the pitcher into her glass.

Is there anyone, besides my own family, who still has formal dinners like this? My grandparents, on Father's side, have these kinds of meals, too, but we rarely visit them since they live all the way up in Sacramento.

Father lifts his fork and pierces a potato. "Did you pick up my suit from the dry cleaners today, dear?"

"No, I'm sorry," Mother says as she sets down the pitcher. "I'll make sure to get it tomorrow."

Father noticeably bristles, and now that I think about it, my grandparents are that way with each other, too. Sometimes, I wish things could be more relaxed at home.

"So, how's ballet going, honey?" Mother asks.

Deanne glances up from her fingerling potatoes and finishes chewing before daintily wiping the edges of her mouth with the cloth napkin, just like Grandmother had taught her to do. "Fine."

Mother smiles. "Do you know what ballet you'll be doing yet?"

"Yes. We're going to learn *Giselle*. Miss Val played some of the music for us on Saturday. It's really beautiful." Deanne finds herself sitting up a little straighter just thinking about ballet.

Father clears his throat, so she turns toward him respectfully.

"Will you be playing the lead role now that you've been in the Advanced class for over a year?" His dark eyes rivet on her.

She hears Mother cough warningly, but his gaze doesn't leave her.

"Well, not exactly," Deanne begins. "Randi is going to be Giselle." She quickly tells him that she gets to dance two roles, but he interrupts her.

"She's not the usual one, is she, dear?" he asks, furrowing his brow toward Mother.

"No. Bree's not there anymore. Is she, Deanne?" She folds her hands in her lap.

Deanne quietly sets her fork down onto her plate. "No."

"Then why aren't you moving up to dance the part?" He shakes his head and stares out the window behind Mother.

"Randi's older than me, Father. Besides, I haven't been in the Advanced class as long as she has."

"That's beside the point, Deanne!" A few beads of sweat glisten on his forehead. "Lord knows I've paid enough money to that place over the years." The legs of his chair scrape the floor as he pushes away from the table and leaves the room.

Deanne looks down at her plate, still half-full, and suddenly feels queasy. "I can't eat anymore. I'm sorry, Mother." *I know it's not my poor Mom's fault that the perfectly decent meal is ruined.*

"Don't worry about it, honey. Your father doesn't really understand the whole ballet thing. He just wants what's best for you. And I want you to know that I'm very proud of you."

"Thank you. May I be excused?" She just wants to go up to her room and be alone.

"Yes, you may." Mother stands up stoically and begins clearing the dishes.

Upstairs, Deanne shuts her bedroom door, flops down on the bed, and pulls a pillow over her head.

I'm sick of always being a failure in Father's eyes. Nothing I do is ever good enough.

He makes her think that she always has to compete with everyone else, even if she feels guilty doing it. And it certainly doesn't seem to help her make friends. Sometimes he's even condescending toward Mother. Like if the pot roast is too well done or they run out of his favorite trail mix that he takes to work—every single day. *God forbid he'd have to nibble on something else for a change.*

And last semester when she'd gotten all As and one B? She thought he'd say, "Good job, Deanne! I'm so proud of you."

But no. Instead, he'd said, "What happened here, Deanne? Why didn't you get an A in math?"

Didn't he know how hard math is for me? Apparently not.

She was amazed that she'd done as well as she had. In fact, she was sure she'd failed the final, but in the end, she'd gotten a B! But instead of feeling happy and proud, he'd whittled her excitement down to nothing.

She absentmindedly flips the pages of the book lying open on her bed and watches the colorful dragons come to life. *At least they have a reason to spew fire—it's their lot in life. But what is Father's excuse?* The ballet casting is just one more thing, in a long list of things, that made her sulk back to her room, once again, to feel sorry for herself and escape inside her fantasy novels. *Thank the Lord, and Brindle, for those.*

When the bell announces the end of the minimum day that Tuesday, Deanne heads for her locker. Brindle is already there, absorbed in a book.

"Hey. Get your stuff. Let's go. You can read when we get to the library." She looks around at the other students leaving their classrooms and flips her hair back. *I can't wait to be in high school with all the cool kids. These new seventh graders are so immature.*

Usually on Tuesdays, Sophia's mom picks them up and takes them straight to ballet. But today, being a short day, they're going to the library first, as well as for their usual after-ballet visit. All three of them are bookworms and *love* going to the library. They hurry out to the parking lot, where their friend and her mother are already waiting.

"It's about time," Sophia says, rolling her eyes. "What took so long?"

Sophia's four little siblings argue noisily in the back of the van.

I wish those little brats would shut up. They're always so annoying. "Brindle had her face in a book again," Deanne teases.

"What's new?" Sophia scoffs. "But that book is actually really good."

"It is, isn't it?" Brindle says. "I'm almost finished, but I don't want it to end."

"Well, don't tell us what happens," Deanne says, opening a small jar and dabbing foundation over the mole on her right cheek. "The minute I turn eighteen I plan to get this thing removed."

"You don't need that stuff," Brindle says, turning toward her, removing her glasses and putting them in the case. "It's like a beauty mark."

"She's right, Deanne," Sophia's mom says, looking into the rearview mirror. "You're such a pretty girl."

"Are beauty marks a cultural thing, do you think?" Brindle asks, matter-of-factly.

"Oh, probably." She returns her focus to driving the carpool then scolds her little charges in the back, with rapid Spanish Deanne can't understand. The three middle schoolers try to ignore the racket and carry on their own conversation.

How is it that Brindle seems to know so many things and be so comfortable conversing with grownups? I usually worry they'll see right through me and read my mind or something. Keeping such conversations short and to the point is much safer.

When the car stops, they thank Mrs. Hernandez for the ride and climb out of the van.

Mrs. Hernandez calls through the open window, "Have fun, my three musketeers!"

They wave back at her before entering the library through the huge, stained-glass entryway, and find an empty table near the back. Brindle immediately opens her book.

"Oh, no you don't," Deanne says. "I want to know what you thought of youth group. You never told us."

"Well, it was okay, I guess. It's just not my thing. I thought I should check it out for myself, though. Thanks for inviting me."

Deanne's mood deflates. She had actually given some hope to the prospect of having her friend join her, on a regular basis, on Wednesday nights. It would be a little something extra to look forward to. Sophia is okay, but she's a whole year younger. And she's more Brindle's friend. Cultivating this friendship is important to Deanne's status at the Dance Centre. *If I stay close to Brindle, maybe I'll get to dance the lead role sooner.*

Sophia says, "I don't get a choice. My mom makes me go. But usually it's fun, I guess."

"Yeah, I like it," Deanne says. "Don't you want to go to church sometimes? I mean, we all want to be saved, right?" *After all, I am genuinely concerned about my friend's salvation.*

Brindle sets her book down on the table, closing it thoughtfully, and Deanne takes a shaky breath, watching her.

Oh no. Here it comes.

"Okay, guys. You know the deal. We don't try to convert each other. Remember? We each believe differently, and that's okay. We can still be friends. Right?"

Deanne feels Brindle's strong gaze under those full, dark eyebrows. She kind of knows she's overstepped a little, but is willing to chance it for the greater good. But both she and Sophia drop it when the librarian walks over with an index finger poised over her closed lips. The three girls nod to her, ending their uncomfortable conversation, and move on to neutral territory, their latest readings about dragons.

When the *barre* work begins, Deanne watches Brindle, Sophia, and Paige, as new *pointe* dancers, hold the top metal pole tightly. When it's time for *relevés* on one foot, they grip with two hands while facing the *barre*.

I'm not using the barre, and notice that it's still much easier on my right foot than the left, but I'm working hard to get stronger.

"You can't do that, Paige." Miss Val comes over, wagging her finger at her foot.

"Do what?" she asks.

Miss Val pauses before snagging a teaching moment. She faces the *barre* to demonstrate. "I want you all to watch and tell me which is the right way to do a *relevé*. This is number one," she demonstrates. "And here's number two." Again, she *relevés*. "Well? Which one is correct?"

No one answers. So Deanne states the obvious.

"The first is better. The second time, you went up before your leg was straight."

"That's correct. Good job, Deanne." She demonstrates again, making her point clear. "Okay? Let's not anyone do it that way or the ballet cops might come in and give you a bad ticket. After all, it's illegal you know." Miss Val often threatens these imaginary tickets from the "ballet cops," which always bring snickers from the students.

They repeat the exercise, and Deanne uses the repetitions to strengthen her ankles.

Ballet cops. My foot. Dancing en pointe is harder than it looks. Compared to everyone else, I must look like a pro. Except maybe to Randi.

After finishing at the *barre*, they sit down to stretch on the floor. Miss Val is going over her notes in the corner by the stereo. Todd, one of the high school's boy dancers, stands and begins rolling up his t-shirt sleeves to admire his biceps in the mirror.

What a clown.

"Hey! I think my muscles are getting bigger. What do you think, girls?" He nods to each of his skinny black arms.

The class giggles, and Deanne's interest is piqued.

Jack says, "Well, I guess in that case they must have been concave to begin with, seeing how miniscule they are now."

It's surely not meant as a mean comment. The two of them constantly harangue each other, but it's all in fun. Laughter fills the room. Deanne presses her shoulders back and lifts her chin, primly.

Paige gets up and steps in front of Todd, taking his hands and placing them on her hips. "Ready?" she asks.

"Always," Todd says, prepping himself in a hilarious, off-kilter *plié* in fifth.

Paige jumps straight up in a *soubresaut*, throwing her arms upward. "Wee!" she giggles.

After he puts her down, they both laugh hysterically and she says, "I think you *are* getting stronger."

The entire class loses it and joins in their raucous laughter. But Deanne just wishes she's the one getting picked up and carried around. Partnering and dancing in a *pas de deux* is so romantic. She can't wait to get older and partner. However, she smiles anyway and giggles along with the group.

"Whoa. That's a tricky lift," Jack says.

The dancers, including Miss Val, who's walking back from the stereo, all chuckle good-naturedly. That's one of the really cool things about this studio. Everybody gets along. At least they do their best to. Miss Val makes sure of it.

The dance of the Wilis music begins and the students scramble to their places. Annie, as Merthe the Queen Wili, leads the other Wilis in a dance around Todd, making him dizzier by the second as the music reaches a crescendo. It doesn't seem like he even has to pretend that the Wilis are getting the best of him. He falls down repeatedly, and eventually to his death. Not really Todd, of course, just his character, Hilarion.

"Well done, Todd!" Miss Val calls, clapping her hands enthusiastically. "And you too, Wilis," she says, laughing. "Your next target is Jack."

They all cheer as Jack holds up his hands in mock protest, and the following segment of music cues them on to the next dance. Deanne keeps her eye on Randi, and an interesting idea occurs to her.

What if I learn Giselle's part, too? Actually really work on memorizing it? Just in case.

During the last ten minutes of class, when Randi and Jack practice one of their duets, Deanne marks the steps that Randi executes.

This is going to be tricky, but at least I can try.

"I'll see you all on Saturday for class and rehearsals," Miss Val says, as the students put on their street shoes and head out the door.

Deanne's mom picks up the three musketeers, as everyone calls them now, to chauffer her charges to the library for two hours before they'll come back for their contemporary class this evening. Tuesdays are exciting for Deanne. Two dance classes in one day, and a trip to the library with her friends sandwiched in between.

Miss Val comes out to thank Deanne's mom for driving the girls.

Brindle is lucky to have such a creative, artsy mom. Their family life seems so much more relaxed and free than mine does. Could it be because I'm an only child? Being raised by a strict, conservative father? I love my parents, but sometimes it might be nice not to feel on edge all the time. Plus, it might be fun to have siblings to break up all that quiet.

4

THE BOLSHOI BALLET COMES TO TOWN

Randi

Push down through the supporting foot in a pirouette—instead of concentrating on the rise.

Randi wakes with a start to the alarm ringing on her dresser, but she can't quite reach the blasted thing. She pulls and pulls on the sheet that's twisted around her legs. Finally, she kicks free and presses the snooze button. *Just five more minutes to snuggle underneath the blanket and get warm.* Last night was a bear. She couldn't shut off her mind and now the worries return.

How on earth can I possibly pull off dancing the lead role in Giselle? It will be so many steps to remember. And not just lots of steps, but really hard ones!

Miss Val had told her that with extra work she would be ready. Randi desperately hopes she's right, but isn't confident at all. In fact, she's scared silly.

The beeping returns and forces her to sit up and yawn—again and again. "Another day in which to excel," she tells herself. But it's not helping to build her confidence.

❧

David is being his usual, annoying self this morning— leaving a trail of milk along the front edge of the kitchen counter.

"Why don't you ever clean up after yourself?" Randi asks. She tears off a couple of paper towels from the roll and shoves them toward him.

"I was going to clean it up." He takes them from her and wipes the surface haphazardly. "Hey, guess what I found out."

"No telling. What?" Randi says flatly, putting a hand on her hip.

"The only reason you got to move up in ballet, to be Giselle," he says, making air quotes, "is because of what happened to Bree."

"Do you know what happened to her?" *This piques my interest in spite of his irritating, condescending tone.*

"She's pregnant!" He stops for dramatic effect and raises his eyebrows.

Randi freezes. She can't move. *That can't be true.* "No way. Are you sure?"

David leans back against the cabinet, softening his demeanor. "I'm afraid it is."

Randi shakes her head and stares at him. "How do you know? I mean, how'd you find out?"

"My friends and I saw her get into her car at school. And she's kind of big, you know? And someone heard that she's doing independent study now, to finish her senior year. None of us knows who the dad is though."

"I can't believe it!" *I stand there, bracing myself on the kitchen island, leaning onto both hands.* "How can that be? I feel so bad for her."

"She was a good dancer, too, huh?" David is actually being nice.

"Yeah. A super good dancer." Randi catches a glimpse of a huge, red apple in the bowl by the sink. *It looks pregnant, too.* "You know, we probably shouldn't tell people about it. I don't want to be the ones to spread gossip, you know?" She doesn't know Bree very well, but she likes her and doesn't want her reputation to be completely ruined—at least by them.

"Okay. I guess you're right on this one. I gotta go." He grabs the engorged apple from the bowl, tosses it in the air, catches it, and takes a bite as he heads out with the car keys.

Randi absently pours cereal and milk into a bowl and slices a banana on top, while trying to picture the image of Bree, pregnant. *But she has the perfect ballerina body and is such a beautiful dancer. How could she have let this happen?* So many questions swirl through Randi's mind, but by the time she leaves the kitchen she's decided not to let herself dwell on them, and instead, focus on being the best possible Giselle she can be. That's a tall order, to be sure.

That evening, Randi and Paige gobble slices of pizza while Mom scurries around the kitchen tidying up and putting dishes in the dishwasher. Dad's reading in the living room, and David is out with friends.

"Are you girls ready? It's already 6:30."

"Yeah, Mom. I just need to grab my coat. We'll meet you at the car," Randi says before swallowing the last of her glass of milk. She takes a napkin from the table, wipes her mouth, and heads for the trash can with their paper plates and the pizza box.

"I'm so excited!" Paige says, her blonde curls fastened with barrettes on each side of her face. "This will be the first professional ballet I've ever been to."

"Well then," Randi says. "I'm super glad that we can do these kinds of things together."

"I don't get out much since my mom works so much. And her clients can be a little needy sometimes, you know what I mean?" Paige gets a faraway look in her eyes. "Plus, it's just the two of us."

Randi nods and hands her a sealed bottle of water. "Ready? Let's go."

On the way to downtown San Diego, Randi sits in the front seat next to her mother. She and Paige have been looking forward to this for a long time.

"Thank you so much, Mrs. Boles, for bringing me along with you. I wonder what the costumes will look like. Oh, and isn't this the ballet where the ballerina does, like, thirty-two *fouetté* turns?"

Randi laughs at Paige's exuberance. "It is indeed."

She watches her mom glance in the rearview mirror. "You know, we're sitting way up in the balcony. The seats aren't all that great."

"In the nosebleed section," Randi adds. She's been to many ballet performances over the years.

"I don't care where we sit as long as I get to go," Paige squeals. "My mom even let me get this new dress to wear. Oh, and my sister called this afternoon and said she's coming home from college for Easter. I can't wait to see her. My dad might even come down from LA when she's here. I didn't get to see him last month. He had to work or something."

Randi is amused by her friend's talkativeness and turns around as she's straightening the skirt of her pretty purple dress.

"I'm glad you're so excited, Paige. It's fun to get an evening out to the city once in a while. And that's great news about your sister. She's still at UC Berkeley, right?" Mom smiles and merges onto the freeway.

"Yeah," Paige says. "I'm thinking of going there, too. But who knows?"

"You still have some time to think about it." Mom then asks Randi how rehearsal had gone earlier that day.

"It was tiring," Randi says. "But I've got a second wind now." At least she got that catnap on the sofa this afternoon, with her furry companion, Butch. "I'm still trying to catch on to that tricky sequence after the jump lift." *No matter how hard I concentrate, I still haven't memorized all the steps yet.*

"That was an amazing lift you guys did today," Paige says. "For a minute, I was worried Jack would drop you."

"I know, right? But I think we're getting it down a little better now. The first few times we tried it Miss Val had us do it on the mat. She's really careful like that," Randi says, looking out the window at the mishmash of freeways and hotels that make up Mission Valley.

"Well, I, for one, am glad of that. And having watched so many of your classes and performances, I appreciate and value how conscientious a teacher she is," Mom says.

Randi turns to look at her. "Yeah, Miss Val's pretty amazing." She stretches her legs and rotates her ankles, a habit she's developed to keep from getting stiff. "I just wish I could remember all the steps better. I feel like such a moron sometimes."

"You're not a moron. Don't be so hard on yourself," Paige says.

"Paige is right, Randi. Give yourself more credit. You're a wonderful dancer."

"Just not wonderful enough to remember all the variations."

As they walk into the foyer of the theater, Randi watches her friend look around in awe. It gives her new eyes to look through. The massive chandelier glitters with a million lights.

"Wow, they even serve champagne here?" Paige asks.

Servers glide through the crowd carrying trays of champagne flutes filled with sparkling liquid. A red carpeted staircase spirals upward to the balcony, where men in black suits and ladies wearing form-fitting dresses stand around having polite conversations.

"Pretty fancy, huh?" Randi responds and, of course, notices the obvious ballet students as well. Everyone seems to be in another dimension. Not the normal one, but a magical world of dancers and ballet aficionados.

After visiting the fancy restroom and settling into their seats, the girls wait for the performance to begin. The lights dim and the orchestra starts to play; Randi closes her eyes and smiles, allowing herself to be carried into the enchanted story of *Swan Lake*.

The curtains open onto the scene of Prince Siegfried's coming of age celebration and she can sense the words of the story—as if an imaginary narrator is speaking in her mind. The festive mood comes across in the dancers' movements and faces, as well as from the music. Beautiful young maidens dance around the prince and vie for his attention. By royal obligation, to become king, he must choose a wife at the upcoming ball.

Randi notices when a line of male dancers run forward together, leaping in a *grand jeté,* that one of them performs the movement without jumping. He opens his arms in a simple *port-de-bras,* just like the others, but without the leap.

"Did you see that?" she whispers.

"See what?" Paige asks.

"That one guy didn't do the leap. Maybe he's injured." *Perhaps I notice these things more since I've taken ballet longer than Paige. After all, accidents can happen, even in a company as prestigious as the Bolshoi.*

As the festivities wind down, Randi's inner narrator returns. Siegfried realizes his carefree days are nearing an end. In the next scene, he seeks solace by himself on the banks of a mysterious lake. It is here that he falls in love with Odette, a beautiful young maiden who fell under the spell of the evil sorcerer, Von Rothbart. Her fate is to be a white swan. Only in the hours of night is she permitted to resume her human form.

At intermission, the girls go back out to the balcony above the lobby and get drinks from the water fountain in front of the restrooms. Randi leads the way over to the railing to look down at the mingling crowd below and gaze at the chandelier again. She's thinking about the story when she notices a petite, pregnant woman in a tight black dress.

"It sure is pretty, isn't it?" Paige says.

"What?" asks Randi.

"The chandelier, silly. I know. You're still thinking about Prince Siegfried and his undying love for Odette," Paige says, jostling her friend's shoulder.

Randi pulls her focus away from the crowd below. "Well, sort of. But actually I found out something rather interesting today." She leans closer to Paige. "You know how Bree just seemed to disappear from ballet?"

"Yeah," Paige says, turning in interest.

"Don't say anything, but I heard she's pregnant."

Paige gasps and covers her mouth. "Oh my gosh! Poor Bree!" Her eyes are huge with shock. "That would explain it," she finally says. "Where did you hear it?"

"From David. He told me this morning," Randi says.

"Your brother? How did *he* find out?" Paige puts her hands on her hips and leans in to listen.

"He said a couple guys on the soccer team saw her. I guess she's doing independent study to finish school." Randi shakes her head, still in disbelief. "She was such a good dancer."

"I wonder who the guy is. Did he hear that?" Paige stares at her intently.

"No. I feel so bad for her. I mean, I'm glad I get to be Giselle, but still." *Hopefully, that doesn't sound too lame or stuck up.*

The lights flicker to signal the audience back into the theater to take their seats. The girls make their way by following other ballet patrons. Randi hopes she and Paige will be able to focus on the ballet after discussing the shocking news about Bree. And as the music begins, they are, indeed, pulled back into the enchanted world of fairy tale love and magic spells.

At the ball, Von Rothbart, who is an uninvited guest, brings the ravishing, young Odile. She looks just like Odette, thinks the prince. But she is not. As the evening progresses, the prince becomes smitten with Odile, the black swan, completely convinced that she is actually Odette. As he announces that he has chosen her to become his bride, the throne room plunges into darkness. The real Odette appears before the assembled group and Siegfried realizes he has been the victim of a terrible plot. Odette weeps. Grief-stricken, Siegfried rushes out.

Randi has grown accustomed to having a narrator at their own story ballet performances, speaking between acts, so she figures that must be the reason for this *inner telling*. But whatever, it helps her keep track of what's going on.

In the next scene, at the lake, a great storm rages. Siegfried begs Odette's forgiveness. As dawn approaches, Von Rothbart appears. He threatens them menacingly before they throw themselves into the lake. With this ending, the evil spell is broken.

The audience applauds wildly as the curtain closes and then reopens for the extended bowing of dancers.

"Look, Paige. There's the guy who didn't leap. He's bowing off to the side. I bet he twisted his ankle or something," Randi says. It must have happened during the performance. *But when? It's a mystery.*

"Huh? Yeah, maybe." Paige is smiling and clapping her hands loudly.

Randi stands with the entire auditorium to add her appreciation for the wonderful performance. When the house lights come up, she follows her mom and friend out of the theater.

"That was wonderful!" Paige says breathlessly. "Thank you so much for bringing me with you. I loved it."

"You are most welcome, Paige," Randi's mom says. "We'll have to include you the next time we venture into the city."

"Yes, we will," Randi says. "I wonder what ballet they'll perform next year. Or if they're even coming back." *All of a sudden, Mom reminds me of Nana, only younger.* "Hey Mom, wouldn't it be great if Nana could be here and go with us?"

"That would be nice," Mom answers.

The three walk through the haze hovering around the crowd standing in front of the theater, and quicken their pace to the car. The ballet world still has more than its share of smokers.

Randi allows herself to drift into thought as the sedan traverses the city streets. She knows Mom is a little uncomfortable driving at night in the city, but admires her for doing it anyway. *Sometimes I wish I could rally more strength in order to overcome my own fears.*

After a long silence, Randi turns back toward Paige. Light from the street dances across her face in colorful swirls. "Don't say anything about Bree," she mouths to her friend.

Luckily, Paige understands and nods.

It's not a comfortable topic and not one she feels like discussing with her mother right now. So she starts pondering other worries, like the whole learning to drive thing. *Will I ever be able to relax into driving the way grownups do?* Being the one in the driver's seat is still such a new and foreign feeling.

"Hey, Mom? I sure hope driving is one of those things that gets easier with practice, like dance." Although, even now, new steps and combinations require such concentration and practice. But she should have the steps down by now. *The harder I concentrate, it's like, the worse it gets.*

"You'll be fine," Mom says.

"Those dancers in the performance tonight were so good, so talented. Who am I fooling? There's no way I'll ever be as good as those professional dancers. Hah! And what is it with Deanne copying my steps all the time?"

Mom yawns at the same time Paige does, then says, "Just relax and enjoy the view, Randi."

Bright lights and neon signs light up the downtown area even though it's almost midnight. Driving up Sixth Avenue toward Hillcrest and passing Balboa Park, Randi can make out lumpy figures lying in the semi-darkness—San Diego's homeless. They enter the freeway and pass by big box stores, hospitals, hotels, and beacon lights waving in the night. Just then a Jaguar speeds by in the fast lane.

"That's a cool car!" Paige yells, and adds with a touch of sarcasm, "I'm impressed, aren't you?"

"No," Randi's mom says. "I can't say that I am."

"I'm just joking, Mrs. Boles. I wouldn't be caught dead riding with that idiot."

Randi laughs at her friend's quick choice of words and says, "Mom, you know, David drives too fast. He even squeals the tires sometimes." This isn't the first time she's talked to her parents about her brother's driving.

"Not like some of the other kids at school, though," Paige says defensively.

I think Paige sort of likes my brother. I don't see why, though.

"Well, I should hope not. I'll talk to him again," Randi's mom says, yawning. "What a wonderful evening it's been."

Randi finds a classical station on the radio and then, tingling sensations dance down her legs. The melody is one from *Giselle*.

"I recognize that tune," Paige says.

"Yup, me too."

All of a sudden, I remember having to sit through all those boring afternoons and weekends of David's soccer practices and games, and it hits me how lucky I am to have found ballet. It feeds my heart and soul like nothing else and influences practically everything I do or think about.

Before long, they're making their way up the dark mountain road to Nuevo. It was nice to visit the city, but Randi kind of likes living in a small town. Otherwise, she'd probably never get the chance to dance the lead role in *Giselle*. She closes her eyes and drifts into thoughts of castles and princesses and fairy tale romance.

5

STANDING IN FOR RANDI

Deanne

It's not a race!

Deanne enjoys learning the dance of the Wilis. She likes the idea of playing an ethereal ghost who dances men to their deaths and sometimes even envisions one of them being her father. She loves him, but he's too controlling. *Who gave him all the power, anyway? God? Oh yeah. That's what they say in church.*

This world of fantasy allows her to pretend she has more power than she actually possesses. Miss Val's story ballets, which she calls *literature in action,* lead them all into an alternate universe where they can escape. It permeates their spring reality. The effect is magical.

This year, Randi has been assisting Miss Val with the Beginning and Intermediate ballet classes, since Bree isn't there anymore. But today, Deanne gets to fill in for her, because Randi has a dentist appointment right after their class. Everyone knows Randi is interested in someday becoming a professional dancer or a ballet teacher.

That lucky duck gets to learn about teaching dance from Miss Val every Tuesday.

Deanne is excited to take her place, even if it *is* only for one fine March day.

"Sorry I won't be able to go to the library with you guys today. But I'm so excited I get to stay and help your mom," Deanne says, after the Advanced class is over.

Brindle wiggles her arms into the straps of her backpack. "That's okay. We'll see you later in Contemporary."

She and Sophia wave back at her and follow the other Advanced dancers out the door.

Deanne decides to keep her *pointe* shoes on to impress the little girls. She dances in front of the Beginning students, demonstrating the *barre* exercises.

Maybe they'll think I'm better than Randi.

When Miss Val isn't looking, she walks around on her toes and watches the little kids stare at her feet in amazement.

"How do you do that?"

"Oh, it's easy once you're an Advanced ballerina and get to wear *pointe* shoes."

Some of the little girls try to stand on their tiptoes.

Miss Val approaches. "No, no. We don't do that without special shoes and you need to be older." She shoots Deanne a disapproving look and begins demonstrating the next exercise.

She steps back into her place, literally and figuratively, nodding demurely. *But I must have impressed the younger students since they always look up to the more advanced dancers.*

Miss Val takes advantage of this by putting on story ballets instead of separate dances in a recital, so the little ones can see, up close and personal, what they're aspiring to.

Deanne takes the Beginners' hands and leads them to the positions where Miss Val wants them to be. They'll be performing in Act One as villagers.

"I need you to skip this way," Miss Val explains. "Toward Batilde. She's the one engaged to the prince. And you follow her, but go around."

Deanne stands where Batilde will be so the children understand they'll be going around a real person. Eventually, they all skip around in the basic directions they're supposed to go. One of them giggles when Deanne grimaces at the end of a *pirouette* and accidentally trips on her own *pointe* shoe ribbon, which has come untied.

"Okay, girls. It's time to try on your costumes," Miss Val announces.

They squeal with delight and follow her over to the *barre*, where the dresses hang. Every year, the kids try on the studio's rental costumes or get measured for new ones to be made by the costume lady. Deanne helps the little girls into the cute little peasant dresses. They're so excited they can't help but twirl around and watch themselves in the big mirrors lining the front wall.

"Look at me! Pink is my favorite color!" One little ballerina spins around on one foot and falls down on her bottom, giggling.

Deanne thinks back to last year, when she danced the part of a princess. She loved that costume and remembers how she wanted to wear that dress forever.

"All right, you. Come back over here, and let's take that dress off and hang it up so it will still be beautiful for our performance, okay?" Miss Val places her hands on the little girl's shoulders and steers her back to Deanne. Then she records the number inked on the inside of the back seam so when concert time arrives, the costumes can be handed out to the correct dancers.

In the next class, Deanne leads the Intermediate students in the dance of the Wilis. These girls are older and know more of the dance routines, so her job is much easier.

Some of them actually can dance pretty well.

"Could you stretch them while I go over my choreography notes? Let's say five minutes or so?" Miss Val asks.

Deanne sits down in front of the group, spreading her legs in a straddle. "Okay, everyone, lay over your right leg first." She tries to sound authoritative, but her voice shakes a little. She sits up straighter and clears her throat.

Miss Val's daughter, Willow, lays her body full-length onto the floor. A heavyset girl named Lisa rolls her eyes and pulls hard on her right foot.

"It's not a contest, girls," Deanne says. "We're all just trying to improve." *There, that sounds better.*

There's obviously tension between her and Willow. The other girls are nice enough, but this "Lisa" girl seems to be trying to compete with the others. *Oh well, whatever. At least Miss Val's here if the girls get too out-of-hand.*

"All right, Wilis. Come get in your starting places," Miss Val says, as she walks to the front of the studio with her notebook. "Deanne, how about if you come up here and dance where you'll be, in your spot for the Wili dance?"

Oh good. The pressure's off. She'll just tell us all what to do now.

It's one thing to dance in front of people, but totally another to talk and teach. Deanne lets out her breath, which she hadn't noticed she'd been holding, and tries to sound more relaxed. "Okey dokey." She *chassés* up to her spot while the young dancers watch. *Now I just need to look better than Randi.*

"I'll be Hilarion for now so you can see where he will be during the dance," Miss Val explains. She dances everyone through the piece, first without music, but with counting. She says it's a good way to learn the steps better and be able to slow down or speed up as needed. Then she asks if there are any questions.

"How will Hilarion die?" asks a brunette, tomboy-looking girl, clumsily twirling around in an inside *pirouette*. She and Willow are besties.

"The Wilis, you guys, and some of the Advanced dancers will make him dance to utter exhaustion. Then he will pretend to die." Miss Val feigns a faint.

"Why don't we die, too, if we're dancing just as much?" Willow asks, lifting her hands in question.

Why hadn't Deanne thought of that? But then she remembers the answer.

"Well, you guys are Wilis. You're already dead. You all died of broken hearts and now seek revenge on men by dancing all of them to their untimely deaths."

The girls giggle and Miss Val starts the music. Each dancer adds her own element of "Wiliness" to the piece in which Hilarion meets his demise. Deanne and the others take turns linking arms and spinning around Hilarion, played by Miss Val. The girls dance in big circles, do *tour jetés* across the diagonal, and leap across the room. Deanne performs her *piqué* turns *en pointe*, showing off to the younger dancers. When the music ends and Miss Val lies on the floor, as dead Hilarion, they all pant and laugh hysterically. Even Deanne gets swept up in the excitement. Helping with the Intermediate class is a lot of fun.

The studio door opens and Mr. Val, as the students refer to him, peeks inside. Miss Val points to him and says, "Shall we perform our Wili magic on him?"

The dancers scream, "Yeah! Can we?"

Deanne watches their teacher hold up her hands to quiet them, and smile at her husband. "No. We'll let him live today, otherwise I'll have to make dinner tonight. He just stopped by to bring Brindle."

Mr. Val waves and slowly backs out the door as Brindle squeezes in under his arm, carrying a stack of books. Deanne helps Miss Val arrange the students back into their places to go over the routine again slowly, with corrections, and then once more with music.

When the class is over, Deanne joins her teacher at the door. "Thanks for letting me help today. I could probably come anytime you need."

"All right, I'll keep that in mind." She pauses. "If you need more to do, would you like to be Randi's understudy? You could learn her parts, since you already seem to be trying anyway—as well as your own, of course."

"Oh, can I?" *I hadn't even thought of that. Actually I had, but I wasn't about to tell anyone.*

"Sure, Deanne. But make sure you know your own dances *very* well, okay?"

"Yes ma'am! I certainly will!" She skips over to take off her shoes and ballet skirt and get ready for Contemporary. This is the last class of the evening. The other students trickle in and Deanne tells Brindle and Sophia about getting to be the understudy for Giselle.

"Can you believe it?" she says, jiggling out of her ballet skirt and letting it fall to the floor.

"Wow," Sophia says. "Pretty cool."

Brindle stands up next to them. "That's nice, but I hope nothing happens to Randi."

The class begins and Miss Val demonstrates while the students mark the movements, and explains, "Marking is like dancing, but not doing it full out. You can learn a routine by gently using your body while watching. This way you can rely on your muscle memory as well as your brain. Both are essential for dancers."

Deanne watches the teacher demonstrate, bending her body forward starting with her head.

"Begin in parallel. Roll down one, two, three, four. *Plié,* five, six. Straighten seven, eight. *Plié* and drop one, two. Straighten up three, four. Rise five, six. Lower seven, eight." Miss Val lowers her heels and comes back to the starting position. "Repeat in parallel second, ballet second, parallel fourth, ballet fourth, and fifth position. And then repeat on the other side. Yes?" She walks over to the corner and turns on a piece of music by *Enya,* and warmups begin.

Teaching and being at the studio this long is hard work. No wonder Miss Val is in such great shape. This class isn't rehearsing anything for *Giselle* because everyone who wants to perform is in other classes as well.

Miss Val claps her hands. "All right everybody, do you all remember our March pattern?"

"Sort of," Sophia says, positioning herself behind Deanne.

"Let's go over it, then. At least in this class we can work on our technique all year without taking the time out to learn parts." Miss Val begins in a Martha Graham sort of contraction and the class follows along.

Deanne's passion is ballet, and she loves being in the story ballets most of all. She's glad she ate a banana between classes, but she's still hungry, and tired, but not nearly as tired as she was before learning that she gets to be Randi's understudy.

What if she'll actually get to be Giselle? Randi only got the lead because Bree isn't there anymore.

This could be my big chance! And where is Bree? She couldn't have just vanished. But no one's talking. What is the big mystery?

Deanne knows she always has to look out for herself to get ahead of others. During class, she's preoccupied with how much the extra practice will make her a better dancer, but even more importantly, will put her in place to overtake the lead role, in case something happens to Randi. She'll learn that girl's part as well as her own *and* be in the right place at the right time.

That's bound to make my father proud!

6

BEING GISELLE

Randi

Dance with the grace of a cat.

Racks of leotards, tutus, and costumes greet Randi and her mother when they walk in through the glass door of the dancewear shop. Bright light reflects off sequins, and pop tunes reverberate throughout the space. Randi heads toward the back wall where the *pointe* shoes are displayed, while her mother parts a row of leotards and studies the assortment. The scent of new satin mesmerizes Randi as she lifts one pretty pink shoe after another, running her fingers around the stiff toe boxes. She's finally found a brand that works for her wide feet, but she still likes looking at all of them.

The familiar salesclerk walks toward the back. "Hello, how are you? Do you need another pair already?"

"Yeah, I do. It's good to see you again. I'm dancing the lead in *Giselle* and my newest ones are already starting to get soft." She holds up her favorite one and asks, "Do you have this in a size seven wide?"

"I'll go check," says the young woman with a diamond stud in her nose, before disappearing through the curtain leading into the back of the store.

Randi turns to look at a colorful poster displayed behind the desk. The Degas print of a group of ballerinas milling around a studio always projects happiness for her. But this time, it comes with a tinge of fear. Now that she's moved up the ranks, so to speak, and is gearing up to the challenge, she finds that being top dog is overwhelming. No matter how hard she tries, she absolutely cannot learn the difficult variations that are required to perform as Giselle. They're way too hard. *When will Miss Val just give up on me and have Deanne take my place?*

"Hey, Mom. I'm thinking I should get two pairs so we don't have to come back so soon." *That's it, just pretend I'm confident.* She wants to feel like a real ballerina talking about going through so many *pointe* shoes. It has taken a lot of blisters and sore feet before finding the right ones, but she still needs to try them on.

The clerk returns with an open, tissue-filled box containing two shining beauties lying delicately within. Randi can't help but take a little whiff when she receives the box. She sits down on the bench and presses her pointed foot into the unforgiving shoe, stands up, and puts her pointed toe weight into the box so the saleslady can squeeze the material together at her heel.

"How does it feel?" the clerk asks.

"Okay. Let me try the other one, too, please," Randi says.

They go through the same procedure with the other foot, and then Randi walks flat-footed around the shop so the stiff shoes won't slip off her heels. By now, with her experience, she can sense how they will feel once the ribbons and elastics are sewn on.

"I like them," Randi says, reaching down to feel the sides of the box on each shoe. She wants to make sure the widest part of her feet have enough room. They are as comfortable as new *pointe* shoes can be, which isn't saying much. They are rigid and tight, but probably all right. This brand has served her well. She remembers trying on her first pair, three years ago, and the excitement she felt. Even now, as "a veteran," that ecstatic twinge still surfaces.

"They're so pretty," her mother says.

"Not for long. It's too bad they can't stay this nice," Randi says, admiring their new pink sheen.

"Would you like the wide or narrow ribbons and elastic?" the woman asks.

"Definitely wide. On both counts," Randi says, packing the shoes neatly back into the carton after taking another whiff. "Nothing like the smell of new *pointe* shoes."

"That's for sure." The clerk pauses and looks at Randi. "I love your hair. It looks different than last time." She leans forward and squints to study it more closely. "It's such a rich brown color. Is it natural?"

Randi pulls a strand of her long hair to the side and looks at it. "The brown is, but I highlighted it with burgundy." She twirls it around her finger, scrutinizing it. "It did turn out pretty well, I think."

"Yeah, you can hardly tell."

Her mother lays a credit card on the desk and finishes the transaction. As they walk out of the store, she asks, "So, what would you like for lunch, Giselle?"

"How about a salad?"

"That sounds perfect," Mom says.

Outside, heavy grey clouds hang low, and it's starting to sprinkle. After putting the new shoes in the car, the two of them walk quickly across the parking lot to Olive Garden. In moments like this, Randi feels such camaraderie. She loves her mom. She even likes her.

"Hey, Mom? I'm glad we got to do this together today."

Mom smiles at her. "Me, too. I realize your school and dance schedules are getting busier. I'm just happy we can still do this sometimes, plus have dinners together—usually."

"Yeah. And I'm super glad Nana is coming to our performance."

"She hasn't missed one yet."

Randi sits in her sophomore English class twisting her pencil in her ponytail while Paige takes notes. It's a sunny afternoon in mid-March and Randi finds herself having a case of spring fever. She watches the leaves flutter in the breeze and drift by the open door of the classroom. The teacher announces the next book they'll be reading.

"*Pride and Prejudice* is a novel by Jane Austen. It was first published in 1813. How many of you have already read it?"

A few hands drift up.

"How many of you have at least heard of it?" Mrs. Goldberg scans the room.

Many raise their hands, but not Randi. She's too distracted watching the trees outside.

"Very well then. This story follows the main character, Elizabeth Bennet, as she deals with issues of the times. Things like manners, morality, upbringing, education, and marriage, all in the context of British high society." The short, round teacher lifts her focus to the back of the room. "We'll have a discussion on the first fifty pages next Tuesday, a week from today. Oh, and I'll give you the details for your essay next week."

That brings her back. Randi squirms at the thought of having to write yet another essay for this class.

What the heck? This must be the third or fourth one already this year. Ugh.

She remembers having to write a persuasive essay for her parents, back in second grade, when she wanted to get a kitten. Her mom had insisted that she needed to show them, in her best writing, the reasons why getting a cat would be a good idea and how she planned to take care of it. *That was so hard.* Writing has never been her strong suit, but luckily Nana was there visiting and secretly helped her write it. Even so, there were many revisions involved and it was sheer torture, as far as she was concerned.

Randi became enamored with cats from the first time she'd visited Nana in Hawaii and seen all those cute kitties clamor around the food bowl every evening. Some of them even let her pet them. Cats turned into an obsession. Her bedroom transformed into a *Hello Kitty* shrine, with the trademark pictures on sheets, comforter, clothes, purses, you name it. She thought back to the happy day when they'd brought Butch home, after successfully submitting her essay to Mom and Dad. He was *so* cute and his meow *so* tiny. He was irresistible and she couldn't help but want to become a cat herself. She meowed at people, painted whiskers on her cheeks, wore cat ears on her head—anything to make her more like a cat.

Now, she rolled her eyes at the thought of how weird she must have seemed to others. *I didn't have that many friends, come to think of it.* Thankfully, this behavior eventually channeled into something less strange—ballet. But maybe it had something to do with the graceful nature of both cats *and* ballet. Anyway, she's happy to fit in better now, although she still does *really, really, really* love cats.

The bell finally rings, knocking Randi out of her reverie, and the students bolt out of the room.

Later, as the Advanced ballet students put on their shoes and lightly stretch, Brindle talks about how much she enjoyed going to see *Swan Lake*. Apparently, Miss Val had taken Brindle, Willow, Deanne, and Sophia to the Sunday matinee.

Randi says, "Paige and I saw it, too. We went on Saturday night. Oh my gosh, weren't the costumes amazing?" She stares longingly toward the back of the studio, where a multitude of the Dance Centre's colorful costumes hang neatly in clear plastic bags.

"Yeah," Brindle says. "I especially liked Odile's. Her black tutu and scary makeup really made her character. Besides, I think the villainous roles are the most interesting and fun."

"She was a great dancer, too," Sophia says, draping her sweater over the ballet *barres* above where she's sitting. "I mean, her cool, villainous role and all. Plus, she was Hispanic, like me." She tosses her long black ponytail over her shoulder matter-of-factly.

Deanne huffs. "Of course. *That's* why she was so good," she teases.

"I think she was a great dancer because of how cat-like she moved," Randi says.

Paige snorts and the rest of them laugh.

Paige nudges Randi. "Just like our latest dancepiration, right?"

"Yes indeed. Dance with the grace of a cat, right?"

"Uh huh. Well, anyway, I think the whole thing was great," Paige says, pulling her grey leg warmers above her knees then folding them down.

Deanne walks over and sits closer to the group. "Is it true? You know, about Bree?"

Randi shoots Paige a questioning look. *Did she tell?*

Paige shakes her head.

Jack says, "Yup. I saw her at Kmart. She's definitely pregnant."

"Wow," Sophia says. "How could she just ruin her life like that?"

"Like what?" Miss Val asks.

Randi hadn't even seen her approach. Sometimes their teacher walked without a sound, so smoothly, almost gliding. *How does she do that?*

"We don't want to gossip here, now do we? And we definitely don't want to make assumptions about whether someone else's life is ruined or just taking a different path. It's not for us to judge. Now, let's dance."

So, Miss Val must have already known.

She claps her hands and motions for them all to get up and get moving.

Randi isn't one to gossip, or to talk negatively about others, but she is curious about the details.

After a short *barre*, it's time to rehearse. Randi begins her Giselle solo when the music starts. She loves all the music in this ballet. Adolphe Adam really outdid himself with the score for this. Within the first few notes, she transforms into her character. She becomes Giselle. Randi floats out to the center as the music directs. After various gesturing, mostly with her arms, she fills out the phrasing.

Miss Val calls over the music, "Randi, lift your chin and amaze the mirror!"

The others giggle.

A simple *port-de-bras*, opening her arms majestically, and turning her head slightly to the right as her chin lifts, conveys a feeling of reverence. During the *balancés*, her hands turn downward and mimic the movement her back foot executes. Her arm, hand, and head motions accent her steps in a way that feels distinguished. She dances her way through the *arabesques*, the *attitude* turns, and yes, more gesturing. That's the easy part. Then come the characteristic hops *en pointe* with her free leg swinging in and out before each landing. And, of course, the *piqué* turn circle. By the end of these, she's always so dizzy she can't see straight. She manages to get through all but the last two turns without looking completely awful—she thinks.

"Not bad, but you'll need to work on those, Randi. Use a stronger spot and keep your core tight. For now, let's practice the hops *en pointe*," Miss Val says and walks over. She helps her up from the end kneeling pose and shows how the landing of each hop has to synchronize with the other foot coming into the ankle. "Like this." Miss Val demonstrates by hopping delicately, swinging her beautiful pointed foot into *coupé* with each precise landing. "Does that make sense?"

It does. Randi notices how much easier the step can be if she focuses on this aspect of it, and, as always, keeps her core strong and balanced. But she still can't remember all the steps in the Wili dance. *What's wrong with me?*

"Relax, Randi. You'll be fine," Paige whispers as she gets into position for the first Wili dance. "Just be Giselle. You know, the lovesick, weak-hearted girl. You can do it."

Randi can't help snickering, but then says, "I sure don't feel like I can." She scowls into the mirror and assumes her position.

All the while, Deanne dances in the background, mimicking Randi's movements. She actually links the steps together without getting flustered. Deanne continues the hops *en pointe* and navigates the turn sequence flawlessly.

How does she do that and why can't I? What if she learns the whole dance better than me? Will Miss Val give her the part of Giselle and make me a regular Wili? Randi pushes these thoughts aside and forces herself to concentrate.

The first few bars of music provide the intro and they all stand motionless. The beginning dance phrases are easy, and Randi has these down pat, but when the tougher combinations come later, she has to concentrate intensely. She has a separate set of moves while the others dance in unison. *Here it comes.* Two double *piqué* turns, each opening into *arabesque*; a series of non-repeating *soutenu, envoîtet,* and *lame-duck entournants*; and numerous connecting steps and intricate foot work—*en pointe*—which Randi bails on halfway through when she loses her balance. She can't remember what comes next. She drops stride and walks around herself in a circle.

"Grrrrr! I don't know where I am!"

Miss Val stops the music and asks the dancers to start in their beginning positions again. "Randi. Even if you forget the dance you have to keep going!" She throws her arms up and shakes her head. "At this point you can't be doing this. You're developing the bad habit of just giving up when you forget. Don't do that!"

I'm so frustrated and mad at myself I can barely make out Miss Val's words.

"From now on, when you start forgetting I want you to keep going. Make it up! It doesn't matter. But just keep going. You have to break this habit *now*." Miss Val brushes a stray hair from her face and abruptly tucks it behind her ear. "Yes?"

"I'll try," Randi says quietly. *My eyes sting and I try to blink the tears away. Quickly, before anyone notices, I turn around and head to my starting place. During the next run-through I remember a little more, but then have to fill in a long segment in the middle with random chaînes and piqué turns. At last, I get my bearings again and join the group in our shared choreography.*

Mrs. Flanners, the costume lady, comes in just as the Wilis dance Hilarion to death. Todd lies on the floor and sticks his legs up in the air—playing dead. The young Wilis giggle at his antics. He looks ridiculous there on the floor with two bright pink barrettes, which he'd stolen from Annie, clipped into his dark dreadlocks.

After the shenanigans die down, Mrs. Flanners yells, "Bravo for the Wilis!" She waves white clumps of sticks in the air. "Look what I found at the craft store! Will these work for scenery, Miss Val?"

"Those are fabulous!" the teacher exclaims. She takes a bunch and examines them closely. Quietly she mutters, "Wili weeds." Miss Val has that devious-looking grin she gets when a creative spark takes over. Most of the Advanced kids know it well. Often something unique and special to the plot or the choreography will be concocted in these moments. "They're perfect. I think each Wili should carry a handful. Aren't they great?"

"Wili weeds, huh?" Mrs. Flanners says, sitting down at the desk chuckling. The kids giggle and she says, "So, who's first?"

Randi swallows her feelings and walks over to get measured first since she has to stay and help with the next class. Mrs. Flanners always asks for their favorite color in case she'll be able to use it in the garment. Of course, Giselle's will naturally be blue. The woman is a long-time friend of Miss Val's and wants everyone to be as happy as possible in their theatrical attire. As the Beginning class is coming in, she leaves and announces she'll be back in an hour. Randi watches the costume lady weave her way through the children coming in the door and overhears Deanne talking to a Beginner.

"Yes. I'm actually a better dancer than Randi, but it's her turn to dance the main part."

What? I can't believe Deanne would say such a thing, even if she is picking up some of the Wili steps quicker than me. And she's younger!

Insecurity creeps down her spine again, making her disheartened and ready to give up. Randi needs bolstering; when she sees Paige outside, still waiting for her ride, she squeezes out the door. The crisp air stings her damp eyes as she approaches.

"What's wrong?" Her friend can always read her.

Randi closes her eyes and takes a deep breath, pulling the coolness into her lungs. But she's already cold, at least toward Deanne.

"Deanne just put me down in front of the Beginners." She shakes her head in disbelief. "And did you see her totally dancing my parts? I think she's actually trying to *steal* my role, not just be the understudy. I hate her."

Paige is half-a-head taller than Randi and puts her arm over her shoulders. "I really wouldn't be threatened by her if I were you. You're light years ahead of her as a dancer. You know that, don't you?" Her frizzy curls stick out from beneath her green beanie.

An intensifying, deep, growling noise forces them both to look up. Paige laughs as a sputtering biplane slowly descends toward the nearby airport, its outline in sharp contrast to the buttermilk sky.

"I've got an idea!" Paige says, still looking up. She takes Randi by the elbow and leads her farther away.

"What now?" Randi asks, stopping after a few steps, bracing herself for another one of Paige's *wise moments*. Her friend has a way of putting a positive spin on things and perhaps this might be one of those times.

"Let's make a pact. Worrying never does us any good anyway, so hear me out, okay?"

Randi nods and watches the line of cars leaving the studio parking lot. The Beginning class has probably already started and she needs to get back in to help Miss Val. "Okay. Hurry up then."

"Let's agree not to badmouth anyone, especially if they're not around to defend themselves. You know, no snarky comments like those popular girls at school are always making. We can be each other's cops. What do you think?"

"You mean, and hold each other to it?" Randi asks.

"Yes. It's nothing new. We've talked about it before, remember? You know, rise above. Like that airplane we just saw."

Randi can't help but laugh. "Oh, is that what made you think of it?"

"Mm hmm."

They chuckle together and Randi agrees to try. Paige's mom drives up; they both wave and Randi hurries back into the studio.

The Beginners are their usual challenging selves and Randi tries to get the four- to six-year-olds to be in the right place at the right time with the music while executing the correct moves. They can be downright difficult, and she admires the patience Miss Val shows them. She's relieved when that group finishes and the Intermediates come in, followed by the costume lady again.

"Hi again, Mrs. Flanners. Long time no see." Randi sighs at her own lame, sarcastic greeting.

"Same to you, Randi. You holding up okay? You look tired."

"I'm okay." *If she only knew.*

Randi lethargically leads the *barre* warmups while Miss Val goes over her choreography notes and helps Mrs. Flanners measure the girls for their Wili costumes, pulling one student away from the *barre* at a time.

"Hold still, Willow. I can't get my measuring tape around a moving target," the costume lady says before recording the circumference of Miss Val's daughter's head. "This is for your Wili head wreath. Is she always this wiggly, Val?"

"Yes she is. Why do you think I have her in ballet, gymnastics, *and* swimming?" she laughs, fussing with her daughter's unruly blonde hair.

It's nice for Willow to have an understanding mom like that. Randi's seen some of the parents that her own mother, as an educational aide, has to deal with. Willow is hyper and sometimes a pain, but she never sees Miss Val totally lose her temper with her.

After they're all measured and recorded, Randi hands each girl a Wili weed and tells them to keep it in their right hand. They don't have quite as much time that Tuesday to practice their dances since the costume lady has come, but they squeeze in two run-throughs of one of their dances and mark another.

Once most of them have gone, Miss Val asks Randi if she can come early on Saturday to practice the *piqué* turn series in a circle.

"Sure. I need all the help I can get." Assisting with the younger kids has helped renew her spirits.

Randi knows Miss Val has spent more time working with her than she would've with Bree. She feels bad that she can't pick it up as quickly, but grateful that she's been given the chance. Living and breathing the part of Giselle does, after all, occupy tons of enjoyable time. Sometimes Randi drifts off during a lecture or math lesson, finding it more difficult than usual to stay on top of her studies. But she's determined. Dancing this part is too important. She constantly reminds herself. *Vigilance, Randi, vigilance. Stay on top of things. Everything!*

7

PRIDE & PREJUDICE

Randi

There's no such thing as a dumb dancer.
One must be smart to pick up steps quickly.

Randi notices a change in her ability to pick up sequences of ballet steps. After having been so close to giving up on ever learning the dances, she now finds herself drifting through the routines without paying much attention. And then, one day in April, she gets through most of the variations without forgetting *any* of the steps. How can this be? Is it simply because of the sheer number of repetitions she's gone through, or is it something else? Miss Val notices, too. She complements her and suggests that she keep up the good work.

What has she done differently to allow herself to pick up the steps more quickly and retain them? *W-e-l-l—I stopped thinking so much and just let my body go through the motions. Could that be it?* Miss Val has talked about that before.

Technique, on the other hand, is a different story. Randi pulls out of yet another circle of *piqué* turns, not quite finishing the last one on the correct count. Changing her spot with each rotation, using her face as a moving target in the large mirrors, makes her dizzy. *Why is this so difficult?* It isn't that *piqué* turns are tricky or anything, but having to perform smaller circles within a bigger circle presents an extra challenge, especially when she has to do so many in a row, or rather, a circle. She almost loses her footing when she spins too far around and barely prevents herself from falling down, headfirst, onto the wood floor.

"Pull it together, Randi. Don't give up at the end! You almost had it," Miss Val says, stopping the music. "Don't think of that last turn as the end. Try picturing it as the beginning of the next sequence. That might help. And breathe, Randi! You've got to fuel those working muscles with oxygen."

Randi takes a deep breath. She knows Miss Val is right, but she hadn't thought of picturing the phrasing differently. Miss Val also talks about the importance of visualizing and actually engaging the appropriate muscles when you're not dancing, using both mental and muscle memories. Randi walks over to get water from her dance bag and takes a long drink, using the time to think about Miss Val's suggestions.

"Let's try it one more time before the others come in for class. It's going to be a long Saturday of classes and rehearsals," Miss Val says.

This time around, Randi begins the *piqué* turns with renewed zest. By the second to last tour, she starts counting out the next phrase and leads with the last turn. Not only does she finish all the dreaded *piqué* turns, but the following *sauté—tombé—glissade—saut de chat* combo feels like a culminating crescendo!

"That's it!" Miss Val exclaims. "See? You did it!"

Randi jumps up and down, excited. "Finally!"

Brindle, who's sitting under the ballet *barres*, looks up from her book. "Bravo! Oops, actually it's *brava*, I believe."

"See? All you had to do was to get out of your own way, mentally," Miss Val says. "It actually does work sometimes. Good job."

The other students trickle in and get ready for class to start. After a short *barre* and a light, quick stretch, the rehearsal for *Giselle* begins. Randi takes another swig of water.

"Let's start with Randi and Jack's main *pas de duex*. Everyone else, please mark through your dance parts in the back—the movements you're performing behind the duet."

Randi accepts Jack's hand when he offers to help her up, just like a real prince, and they walk over to stage left. Arm in arm, they make their entrance, skipping out to center stage as Miss Val counts the phrases out loud, without music.

"One, two, three, four, five, six, seven, eight—look at each other and smile! Five, six, seven. Tilt your head more to the left, Randi. Four, five—pull her closer. She's supposed to be your girlfriend, you know."

Randi is hyper aware of Jack's proximity and finds it difficult to concentrate. Plus, Deanne is practicing *her* steps in the back of the studio. *Ugh!*

"One, two, three, four, five, one, two. Oops. You guys forgot, didn't you? That's a five-count measure. It's not like the pop tunes. This classical music has variable phrasing you *have* to memorize with the movements."

How embarrassing. I know that part, but his hand is so warm on my back. He lets go, and they run through it again with music this time. Randi notices Jack mouthing the counts. When they get fouled up on the next partnering move, Miss Val stops them and motions everyone over to sit by the stereo. Randi is disappointed when Jack settles next to Deanne.

"It's tricky, I know. But Jack, you can't mouth the counts. Only think them and smile, or whatever." She laughs. "We need to count this piece together. All of you." Miss Val points her finger, gesturing to each dancer in turn. She bends to start the music again and strands of her long blond hair slip from her chignon.

Randi turns her head in time to witness Jack staring at their teacher as she twirls the loose hair behind her ear. She feels a pang of jealousy in the pit of her stomach. *What's that about? Does it not matter that she's in a whole different age bracket? Guys will be guys, I guess.*

The class now counts all together—in eights mostly, but also sixes and fives. Miss Val periodically stops class for a mini music lesson. She's a stickler for musicality. Randi can tell everyone understands the music better now. As the teacher continues to explain, she notices the sun is no longer glinting into the front windows. *It must be afternoon by now.* Through the blinds, she can make out an old man walking to his car. It's easier to see out than in, and she sometimes gets distracted. This is one of those times, but she pulls her focus back inside. As the day progresses, the dancers get through a rough approximation of their parts, so they'll be able to practice on their own when Miss Val is working with someone else.

Randi's relieved when lunch break is finally called and they can retrieve food from their bags under the *barres* near the door. She sits down next to Paige, who's opening a bag of Fritos. "Are you looking forward to the slumber party?"

Paige crunches down on a chip before answering. "Yes, I am. Is everyone coming?"

"Yeah, all the Advanced girls." She leans over and whispers. "I didn't really want to invite Deanne, but my mom made me."

"Well, you kind of have to, don't you? I mean, it would be rude not to. Besides, maybe we'll all bond a little more," Paige says, reaching into her bag again.

"I *suppose,*" Randi says, pulling out *Pride & Prejudice* and beginning to flip through it while eating her tuna sandwich. *Might as well try to get some of my homework done.*

Brindle reaches over and pushes the book more upright to read the cover. "What do you think of it?" She seems unperturbed by the senseless banter all around them.

"It's long," Randi says. "Why? Have you read it?"

"Yeah," Brindle says, chewing her apple. "I read it last summer. I loved it. Jane Austen was an amazing writer. I find her characters intriguing, don't you?"

Is this girl for real? "Well, I'm only reading it because we have to for English," Randi says.

"Oh, I loved that book." Deanne now joins in the conversation. "I love how they're so prim and proper and all." She sits up straight and all of a sudden appears obnoxiously prim and proper herself.

Is she trying to show off?

Sophia adds, "Me too. It took me a while to get into it, but now I'm hooked. Thanks to Brindle. It's taking me a long time and I already had to renew it twice."

She looks too young to read about such sophisticated affairs. "Huh." Randi sits dumbfounded and temporarily forgets to chew her mouthful of sandwich. She looks at Paige, who smiles knowingly at her. "You guys actually read this stuff just for fun?" Randi asks. "When it's not even assigned?"

Paige laughs. "It looks like these middle schoolers are showing us up, Randi. What do you guys think about Mr. Darcy? Doesn't he seem kind of aloof to you?"

Brindle wipes her hands on a paper towel and says, with a feigned British accent, "I think he's distracted with gentlemanly duties and doesn't know how he feels until it's almost too late."

How are these girls so well read? And they can dance!

"Really?" Deanne grabs the book from Randi and starts turning the pages. She stops and looks at Brindle. "I think he's kind of arrogant."

Paige adds, "Well, I don't know how realistic it is that he'd change his mind, just like that, about Elizabeth. But it's all so romantic."

Randi listens to her peers go on about Mr. Darcy and Mr. Bingley. And then continue about the personalities of the young Bennets, Jane and Elizabeth.

"You know what, you guys? I've gotten more information about this story hearing you carry on about it than listening to our English teacher or reading the book myself. It makes this far more interesting than it was before. Thanks." She stands up to throw her trash away, thinking about how she hadn't really known these girls before now. *Things are never quite what they seem.*

Miss Val walks toward the stereo carrying her choreography notebook. "Lunch break is over." Her legs brush the sides of her mid-length, black ballet skirt with each step.

She even walks gracefully. Randi's eyes divert to Jack who, once again, ogles the instructor's subtle actions. *Are all guys so easily distracted?*

The dancers twirl their feet in circles to warm up their ankles; stretch down to the floor with straight legs, pulling heads to knees to lengthen hamstrings; and execute a variety of other quick exercises to loosen up their young muscles. Nobody wants an injury that will prevent them from performing in *Giselle.* Especially Randi.

Jack and Todd practice their rivalry roles over Randi by feigning aggressive attitudes toward one another. Following the musical cues, they push and mock each other. Hilarion tries to warn Giselle of Albrecht actually being a prince in disguise, but to no avail.

Randi smiles. She hears that narrator voice in her head again.

Eventually, Hilarion presents Giselle with Albrecht's sword, after secretly stealing it, proving that he is, indeed, a nobleman already promised to another. Of course, Giselle is horrified when it becomes obvious that it's actually Batilde, who she has, unknowingly, become friends with. Giselle loses it and begins dancing erratically, causing her weak heart to give out. Her mother had warned her about the dangers of dancing, but she can't help herself. The scene ends with Giselle's mother weeping over her daughter's body.

"I'm as lovesick as those silly Bennet girls in *Pride & Prejudice,* aren't I?" Randi sighs from her position lying on the floor. "I'm such a stupid fool," she croons in a whiny voice.

Paige bellows dramatically, "Oh, yes. Indeed you are, my friend."

The dancers crack up over the antics of their classmates, joining in the fake reality until Miss Val calls them back to order. "Good job, all. Now let's get back to work."

The beautiful, lively music of the romantic ballet fills the studio and Randi's head, transporting her to an alternate reality. She and Jack hold hands, with crisscrossed arms, and jump from leg to leg in unison. Front *attitude,* back *attitude,* front *attitude,* *assemblé,* and repeat. This is a fun combination, and it isn't difficult to show joy when performing these movements. Randi's timing in the duet improves, but she still gets nervous when she partners with Jack. The others dance behind them in the village scene, each contributing their own personality to this shared experience. She loves how they all lose themselves in the story and become their assigned characters, while also bringing their own personalities to their parts. This is the magic of the Dance Centre's story ballets. The ballet is developing a life of its own.

8

SLUMBER PARTY

Deanne

*It doesn't matter how anyone else
dances—this is about you.*

Deanne is so excited; she can hardly wait for Randi's ballet slumber party tonight. This is the first year that she and her two friends are invited. They had been too young to be main characters in a story ballet before, but now they're considered part of the group. Finally, they've arrived.

Each year, Deanne has heard, Randi invites the main characters to her house for a slumber party where they stay up late, watch ballet videos, practice putting on stage makeup, and eat junk food. Of course, Randi's mother has assured the other parents, especially Deanne's, that the evening will be properly chaperoned. This anticipated event usually takes place several weeks before their performances.

When Deanne's father drops her off on that warm May evening, she's embarrassed when he grills Randi's mom about the night's plans. She quickly gives him the usual peck on the cheek and says, "Bye, Father," before scurrying off to the kitchen where Brindle beckons her. She puts her chips and dip on the counter and then, thankfully, notices her father leave.

Music plays from the living room speakers and a gentle breeze flutters the white, gauzy curtains hanging in the open windows. Deanne appreciates the warmer evenings that spring brings with it, so on occasions like this she can wear her cute halter top. At least, strip down to it after making sure her parents aren't around.

"Cute top," Paige says, reaching over the fruit plate to dip a tortilla chip in the guacamole. "Where'd you get it?"

"At the mall," she answers, brushing a crumb off her exposed chest.

Deanne admires the skimpy pink top and then tosses her head coolly, sending red curls dancing. She likes doing that, but Randi is staring at her. She wishes she were older, like her, and not still in middle school.

Cheers break out when Randi's dad comes through the kitchen door carrying a huge bucket of fried chicken.

"A little sustenance for the dancers!" he calls.

It smells delicious. Deanne hadn't realized how hungry she was.

Randi takes the lid off and rearranges items on the table to fit everything. "Thanks, Dad."

"There're drinks in the fridge for you guys. Have fun," he says and quickly leaves the room.

"Wow. That's so nice," Deanne says. *I doubt my father would ever be involved like this.* She's working hard to fit into the group tonight and is trying to be extra nice.

Randi clears her throat and announces, "Okay, everybody! I think we're all here now. How about we start the movie? I've got a video of the Royal Ballet performing *Giselle.* My Nana sent it to me. Isn't that great?"

"I'm so excited!" Paige says. "I'm absolutely twitterpated. Your grandma is so cool," she giggles, setting down her glass of water a bit too quickly onto the table, sending a wave over the edge. She grabs a napkin and wipes up the puddle, still laughing.

"Twitterpated? What's that even mean?" Annie asks.

Paige looks at her questioningly. "Seriously? You've never heard it before?"

"No," Annie answers. "It sounds like a heart condition or something."

Deanne laughs with the others, wondering about this funny word, too.

Paige sits up straight, looking like a teacher preparing to teach them something important. "It's from *Bambi.* Owl talks about it. How everyone gets *twitterpated* in the spring?"

"Oh yeah," Brindle says, giggling. "I remember that."

"It means being in love then, doesn't it?" Randi asks.

They all laugh.

"Are you in love, Paige?" Randi asks.

Paige snickers. "No. I just take it to mean *excited*."

They all laugh again and Deanne begins to feel a little more relaxed. "Aren't Jack and Todd coming?" After all, she's worn her favorite halter top this evening.

"No," Randi says, obviously annoyed. "You know there's no way your parents would have agreed to let you come if it was, like, an all-night coed party."

Drat. That's definitely true, but Deanne is still disappointed. The others guffaw and march into the living room carrying paper plates filled with snacks. Brindle and Sophia circle the large island, helping themselves to more goodies. Deanne follows their lead and picks out some chips, French onion dip, and a chicken wing. She and her friends high-five each other with their free hands, happy to be included in this special evening.

"Here's to the slumber party. Let's have fun!" Brindle says, and she and Sophia lead Deanne into the living room to join the group.

After grabbing the remote, Randi plops down on the sofa next to Paige. They listen to the orchestra in the pit begin to play and Adolphe Adam's beautiful symphony fills the room. Deanne watches everyone stare at the screen ready to be transported to another place and time. They aren't just watching any old movie. She knows they're really doing research to bring more into their own dancing. Plus, they're forming a closer bond with their stage family. Deanne can hardly believe that she and her friends are finally part of this cool group. But she still feels a little like an outsider here, waiting to be taken more seriously as an advanced ballerina.

The curtain rises, and the village scene appears. Giselle, in her blue and white peasant dress, smiles sweetly and dances among the others. The brightly lit stage with more festive props and elaborate scenery than their own production will be able to afford adds to the significance of what they're doing themselves. With this ballet being over a century old, Deanne feels like they're part of a historical event. She glances over at Randi, whose face flickers in the light coming from the television.

She's so lucky to get to play the lead this year. But if something happens to her, I'll get to be Giselle. Could it be me? I can only hope.

Annie gracefully leans forward from the armchair to grab a handful of popcorn, but stops herself. She looks like a model in a television advertisement.

"You know, you could eat something," Randi says.

"Oh no, I better not. I ate a whole chicken sandwich for lunch." Annie leans back and crosses her arms over her chest.

"Wow. A whole sandwich, huh?" Paige teases. "I ate a snack before coming and I'm still having some chicken and goodies here. Aren't you worried about starving yourself?"

"I'm hardly starving. Look at me." Annie reaches down and grabs a non-existent roll on her stomach.

"Oh, give me a break," Randi scoffs. "You're so thin."

"And beautiful," Deanne says, smiling enviously.

"Anyway," Annie says. "Do you think we'll be able to pull off this ballet? I mean, make it look like such a fun, colorful festival?"

"Sure we will," Sophia answers, reaching forward and cracking her knuckles. Her dark skin and short stature contrasts with Annie's willowy height and pale complexion, although both are waif-like in stature.

"She's right, you know," Randi agrees. "We always do. It obviously won't be the same as this, but it'll be our own version. Miss Val always does what it takes, doesn't she?"

"We all have to do our best, too, you know," Brindle interjects. "My mom always says that it takes a village."

Paige puts a handful of popcorn in her mouth, accentuating her chubby cheeks. She's not one who particularly watches what she eats and it's beginning to show. Deanne, on the other hand, doesn't ever want to get even five pounds overweight.

As Albrecht and Giselle dance around the screen with the rest of the village, Deanne says, "Doesn't it feel a little weird without Bree dancing the lead this year?"

They all look at her, and suddenly she wishes she hadn't said anything. *But it really doesn't feel right without her.*

"I just hope she's okay," Annie says. "She probably wishes she was dancing the lead, too."

Paige carefully sets her drink down on the coffee table. "I think Randi, here, is doing a fine job with it."

"Well, thanks, Paige. I'm really trying. It's hard. I was super surprised when Miss Val offered me the part. Are you guys upset about it?"

"No. Of course not," Deanne lies. "You deserve it." *Why hasn't anyone bothered to congratulate me about being the understudy?* She sinks further into the couch cushions while everyone resumes their focus onto the screen.

Deanne shudders. *What if what happened to Bree happens to me? But it won't. I'd hate to go to judgment day with that hanging over my head. Unmarried and pregnant?* The thought makes her cringe anyway. She'd heard about other girls getting pregnant while they're still in high school, but Bree is the only one who she's actually met. Deanne shivers again and forces herself to think of something else. But before she can pull her mind away from such thoughts, she promises herself that, *No, that absolutely, will never happen to me. I'm a good girl.*

In Act Two, the scene darkens to the mysterious lake and the ghostly Wilis. Their movements appear fluid and otherworldly. The Queen Wili, as they all like to call Merthe, initiates Giselle into the sisterhood. Even on the television screen, a magical essence permeates the scene. Steam rises out of the lake, obscuring Hilarion's vision when he comes to Giselle's grave. She and the other Wilis appear and begin his dance of death. They also use turns and frantic motions in their choreography.

Deanne sits transfixed in Randi's living room until they're all jolted by a phone ringing in the kitchen. Mrs. Boles answers it and motions for Sophia to come. The girls continue watching while Sophia speaks, in Spanish, with her mother about tomorrow's ride.

Deanne gathers that she'll be taking the three of them to the Dance Centre in the morning for the Saturday class and rehearsals. She wishes she could ride with the older girls instead of Sophia and Brindle.

After several rounds of bowing and curtain calls, the video ends and Randi gets up to retrieve the DVD and turn off the television. The group slowly emerges from the enchanted world of *Giselle* and stands up to stretch. Paige feigns a faint. She dramatically brushes the back of her hand across her forehead and swoops down in a modern dance move to lie on the floor.

"What's that about?" Annie asks. "Are you one of those fair maidens passing out from a weak heart?"

Paige rolls around clutching her stomach, giggling.

"Who spiked the punch?" Brindle asks.

Paige finally rests on her back, in corpse pose. "I don't know why it's so funny, but I don't see why all these women in fairy tales fawn over the men so much. I mean, what makes them so special when it's obvious how sexist, and more than a little stupid, they really are?"

Paige sure uses sophisticated words.

Annie furrows her perfectly groomed, black eyebrows into a comical gesture and Deanne laughs.

Randi nods. "She's right. Even these days, we women are not taken seriously enough." She gathers the dirty paper plates scattered around the living room and disappears into the kitchen.

Brindle removes her glasses to rub her eyes and looks down at Paige, who's still lying on the floor.

"I read somewhere that a woman has to do two to three times the work a man does for only half the pay. That's a huge discrepancy."

Randi returns with bottles of water for everyone. "Hey, I have an idea! How about we go to one of those women's marches? You know, try to do our part?"

Paige sits up suddenly. "That's a great idea! My mom was talking about a big one that's organizing for next year. We should all go."

Randi adjusts her position on the sofa and helps up Paige. "My mom and I have already talked about it. I think it's in January."

"Aren't you worried you'll get in trouble?" Deanne asks. *Why would they even consider such a dumb thing?*

"Get in trouble?" Randi snaps, glaring at her. "For what? Standing up for our rights?"

Deanne shifts uncomfortably in the wing chair. "My father says there are people getting hurt at those stupid rallies and the protestors are just being poor sports." *Aren't these girls worried about getting hurt?*

Both Randi and Paige wear expressions of extreme confusion.

"Have you listened to the news?" Deanne offers. *Maybe they just don't know.*

"What news?" Randi asks.

"Fox News?" Paige blurts out.

Annie *relevés* in a huge second position and stretches out her arms authoritatively. "Now, now girls. Let's not get our panties in a twist over this."

Sophia laughs.

Randi clears her throat and looks over at Paige. "I know it's important, especially these days, to just agree to disagree. But I really do want to go check this out."

"I think my mom's planning to go," Brindle interrupts. "And I want to go with her. In fact, my dad will probably go, too."

I can't believe it. "To a women's march?"

"Yes. To show his support of women's rights."

Paige suggests they all go. At least, everyone who wants to.

Randi screws the cap onto her water bottle and stands up. "Well, there's plenty of time to think about it. It's, like, months away. How about we get back to why we're all here. How about makeup?"

Deanne's glad that someone suggests changing the subject, even if it *is* Randi.

"So who's my first subject?" Annie snickers, bending over and pulling out her makeup kit.

"How about me?" Deanne asks, and *chassés* over to get her face dolled up.

"Or me," Paige says, batting her eyelashes and leaning into a suggestive pose.

Brindle and Sophia laugh and Randi walks over holding a large makeup case.

"May the best artist win!" Randi giggles.

"You're on!" Annie says.

Randi motions for Paige to sit on the piano bench and begins rummaging through her artillery of foundation, lipstick, eye shadow, and mascara.

Deanne watches her begin with a light foundation, probably because Paige has fair skin. Then Annie and

Deanne set up shop in the kitchen. Brindle and Sophia look on as Deanne is transformed into a pale-looking Wili.

"Seems fitting for a ghost, doesn't it?" Brindle snickers.

Sophia nods. "But doesn't she look a little like a clown with her red frizzy hair?"

Ouch. Does she always have to be so direct?

Brindle snorts before patting her friend's fluffy hair. "Yeah. Pretty much."

That's it. Deanne is anxious for a more glamorous look. "Okay, now let's take it off and give me the beautiful face of a desired peasant girl. You know, for Act One." Deanne lifts her chin and proceeds to scrub her face with a towelette.

Annie now begins her task in earnest. She applies a mid-shade of foundation to Deanne's serious face and follows with a pinkish rouge on her cheeks, black mascara for the eyelashes, blue eye shadow, and red lipstick.

"This looks better," Deanne says approvingly. She waltzes into the living room and twirls around in front of the competition. "What do you think of this?" she asks, presenting her made-up face with a dramatic opening of her hands in front of her chin.

"Wow. Pretty nice," Randi says. "What do you think, Paige?"

"Uh huh." Paige looks up through blackened eye lashes.

Randi hands Paige a mirror so she can look at her own new face.

"Ooh. This is pretty good, too." Paige looks up at Sophia and Brindle as they walk in from the other room, and flashes them a dazzling, fake smile.

Brindle studies both girls' faces intently. "I think it's a tie. What do you think, Sophia?"

"Hmm. You both look so different. I can't really tell which one is better. Therefore, I agree. You're both winners." She claps her hands and nods to Brindle to follow suit. "Time for cookies!" she says, *pas de chatting* back into the kitchen. "I made peanut butter- oatmeal- chocolate chip cookies for everyone. They're my absolute favorite."

"They are good," Brindle attests. "I've had them before."

The group descends on the tray of small, round goodies like vultures surrounding a carcass. They may be dancers who generally try to watch what they eat, but they're also teenage girls at a fun sleepover. Cookies trump health food on this occasion. Deanne watches Annie take tiny bites off the cookie she broke in half.

By 11:00 p.m., the girls lay out their sleeping bags around the living room floor.

Randi fiddles with the remote. "You guys gotta check this out. I found it on *YouTube* the other day."

Deanne watches the television screen fill with a large, fake head of a cat. The image broadens and a male ballet dancer's body appears underneath.

"Isn't it way cool?" Randi swoons, staring at the dance. "Watch this." She points to the screen. "See how he moves just like a cat? He's got the personality down, too, doesn't he?"

It's true. The ballet moves the guy performs do look cat-like. Deanne thinks it's kind of weird; however, Randi is all excited about it.

When the clip ends, Randi says, "Okay. Now it's time for 'Center Stage!' It's my favorite movie." She tells them she watches it whenever her dedication to dance needs bolstering.

But Deanne thinks that must be rare. *She's such a diehard.*

Halfway through the movie, Randi looks around at the group of dancers arranged haphazardly in her living room. "It may sound weird, but I like this movie so much and it makes me feel so pumped up afterward. You know, super excited about dancing and my commitment to it."

Deanne notices feeling bolstered as well. "Yeah, I like it, too." This does seem like a perfect way to end the evening.

The following morning comes too early for the girls. Randi's dad opens the swinging kitchen door and yells, "Donuts!"

Randi lifts her head and squeals, "Ooh, rainbow sprinkles?"

"And more."

"And chocolate?" Paige asks sleepily.

"Of course," he says before disappearing again.

Deanne shields her eyes from the bright light coming in through the doorway and groans.

"Up and at 'em," Randi says, tossing her bedroll off and standing up to stretch.

"What time is it?" Sophia asks, pulling the pillow over her head.

Randi's mom walks in and answers. "It's 8:30. Time to get up, eat breakfast, and go dance!"

Randi leaves the room taking her bedroll and pillow with her and Paige heads for the bathroom. Deanne rocks back on her shins and reaches forward, lengthening her back and neck muscles. Her bedding feels warm and cozy, but she gets up, reluctantly.

Annie rolls the pillow in her blanket and deposits it by the front door. "Who needs a ride today?"

Randi returns in her dance clothes eating a multi-colored donut.

She even walks like a dancer. And she eats donuts.

"Paige and I do. That way my mom can have the morning off."

"Is your mother coming to get us, Sophia?" Brindle asks. She's the last one out of bed.

"Yup. She should be here in about half an hour." The hungry dancers finish most of the donuts in the box, leaving a few partials someone had tried, but must not have liked. A whirlwind of activity gets the living room and kitchen mostly cleaned up before they all depart for the Dance Centre to spend another Saturday enveloped in the fairy tale world of *Giselle*.

Deanne yawns, gets into the back seat next to Brindle, and imagines what it will be like to someday dance the lead in one of the ballets. Maybe *Snow White* or *Swan Lake* or *Coppelia*.

9

Prop Building and Rehearsing

Randi

Relax into the moves.

The *barre* exercises have a slow-motion quality this morning after the slumber party. Randi sluggishly moves through the *pliés, tendus, dégagés, rondejambes, frappés,* and *grand battements.* She glances out the large front windows at the cars gleaming in the parking lot; the sunlight reflects off the chrome and sends shards of blinding light onto the wall of mirrors. She moves forward, closing into fifth position, escaping the glare. As Miss Val demonstrates a *port-de-bras,* Randi yawns.

"Am I boring you?" Miss Val asks.

"No. It's just that we were all up late at the slumber party last night."

"We're all tired, Mom," Brindle says.

"I see. Well, try not to focus on it, and you might find yourselves getting a little perkier as the morning progresses." Miss Val starts the music again.

"*We're* not tired, Miss Val," Jack says, his long dark bangs hang enticingly over his vivid blue eyes. "Todd and I weren't invited."

Miss Val laughs along with the class and shakes her head. "Okay already. On with the exercise, class." She proceeds to mark the *fondús* for them.

After the dancers put the *barres* away and finish the center stretching, Jack and Todd go out through the open door while the girls run through one of the Wili numbers. On the other side of the window, the boys nail together Giselle's grave marker, a cross standing on a plywood base. Randi can see and hear them joking around out there and repeatedly has to pull her focus back to the dance. Jack is *very* cute and she realizes how often she thinks about him now. *They're just silly boys,* she reminds herself, but she feels compelled to listen to their relentless banter anyway.

Todd throws his head back and laughs. "Those football players just don't get it, do they?" He mimes an exaggerated touchdown.

Jack raises an eyebrow. "Nope, they don't. This is where the cute girls hang out. In dance, not in their little boy huddle."

The guys carry on and Randi blushes just hearing them.

Todd spins around on his heels and they both bust up.

"Keep it down out there, please," Miss Val warns. "Randi, put your heels down when you land those *changements*! You don't want to wreck your knees."

She counts the last phrasing aloud, slowing everyone down. "Be in the present!" she says. "This is not a place to push the music."

She pauses the piece and asks the class, "Do you remember the place in that other dance where I said to push the music slightly, to make time to finish on that last flourish?"

Randi looks around and watches everyone nod.

"Good. But in this number you have to slow down when the music slows. There's a musical term for this, but the word escapes me at the moment. Oh yes, *ritardando*. That's it. Anyway, it's important to really listen and actually feel the music. It's the only way you can be a great dancer. We must develop a strong musicality and incorporate it into our movements. And by the way, math, you know, is directly tied into music and timing. Believe it or not, math, as well as literature, is important for the well-rounded artist. Okay, end of lecture. Go drink some water. And tell the guys to come in."

Randi nudges Paige and they watch Deanne sit down next to Jack. The red-headed Wili offers the prince a sip of her juice, which he accepts.

"You have nothing to worry about," Paige says, leaning in. "She's just being a little flirt."

Randi tips back her bottle and finishes her water. "I know. Rise above, right? But it feels like she's seriously trying to undermine me."

Paige tosses her container into her bag and raises a warning eyebrow. "Don't even go there. It's so not worth it."

Randi frowns and grabs her flexed feet, leaning her nose down to her straightened knees before getting up. Miss Val motions for Jack to come over for the *pas de deux*. Paige and Brindle go out to help Todd with the props.

Jack shakes out his arms and legs and rolls his head around in circles, creating a sickening popping sound. "Okay, I'm ready," he says.

"Gross," Randi says, snickering.

Jack wears a T-shirt with the trim around the neck and the sleeves ripped out. Randi can't help but stare at his chest hairs poking out. Her cheeks flush hot, and she turns her head to look away. Snapping to, they assume their positions off stage left and skip on enthusiastically when the music begins. They smile at each other, appropriately for their characters in the ballet, while Randi fights to clear her head. Halfway through the piece, they perform the fish dive, as they call it, where he holds her left leg near the knee and his other arm wraps around her waist, dipping her down in front of him into a fish shape. This time, her right hand catches her from falling on the floor when she tips a little more upside down than usual. She quickly straightens her right leg from the *passé* position to prevent herself from falling. Jack maintains his hold to keep her from completely tumbling onto the floor. He lays her down and drops onto his right knee.

"Are you okay?" he asks, crouching down on the floor behind her.

Ugh. "Yeah, I'm fine. At least I was close to the floor before we collapsed." *I must look like such a disaster. Like a puddle on the floor.*

"How about you, Jack?" Miss Val asks. "Is your knee all right? That's all we need is for both of you boys to be lame."

Todd hurt his ankle at school last week, and still favors it, even though the doctor said it isn't sprained.

"Oh yeah. It's good." He stands up and shakes his leg. "See? No problem." He reaches down and offers Randi a hand up.

"Thanks," she says, and he gives her a quick hug. Her heart flutters, but she knows dancers are like that. They have to touch each other a lot, especially while partnering. She's pretty new at this, so it's definitely something she's still trying to get used to. And even now that she has most of her other variations down pretty well, she finds herself growing flustered every time she dances with him.

They practice the maneuver twice with no real improvement and then do the *pas de deux* three more times. In the mirror, Randi can see Deanne dancing her steps—not just marking them now. She notices her understudy pushing the pace of her movements. *Is that on purpose? Maybe it is. That way, she can make sure she knows the choreography without waiting for me to do it. Ugh!*

Deanne's *pointe* work is getting stronger and Randi can't help but feel threatened by it. She'd better try to put Deanne out of her mind—difficult when she's in full view in the mirror. Randi needs to focus on her *own* dancing now. But with each run-through, Randi feels herself growing redder each time Jack picks her up. She starts forgetting their partnering choreography. His warm breath tickles her ears. Their sweat runs together in streams down their arms and Randi keeps messing up in places she shouldn't. *This is so embarrassing. Pull it together, Randi!*

"Miss Val?" Deanne asks.

Randi watches Deanne sidle up to Jack.

"May *I* try? I've been practicing a lot and I think I know how to do it."

I'll bet she does.

"Not now, Deanne. Maybe another time."

Randi's relieved when Miss Val finally announces lunch break. The students grab their money and walk down to the convenience store at the end of the strip mall. Most of them haven't packed food because of the slumber party the night before, so chips, nuts, and drinks will have to suffice. When they return, Randi sees Miss Val unpack a salad before joining the picnic on the studio floor.

"What kind of scenery are we going to have, Miss Val?" Annie asks. She's picking through a cluster of green grapes, apparently the only sustenance she's brought, other than a diet soda.

"We're going to have a backdrop painted by one of the dads in the Intermediate class. It will be the night scene at the lake for Act Two."

"What about Act One?" Sophia asks and rips the top off a bag of Cheetos.

"We already have a village backdrop for that," Miss Val explains, opening a bottle of green tea. "How's Giselle's cross coming along?"

"Good," Todd answers. "It's put together now. Do you want to see it?"

They all go outside and stand around the five-foot-tall prop while Todd proudly presents the cross to the group.

"Truly lovely," Paige croons, reaching over and messing up his hair.

"Not the hair," Todd drawls.

"You're so vain!" Paige teases, and they all laugh.

"Well." Miss Val smiles and changes the subject. "It looks like it's ready to paint. I have some whitish-gray paint in the back of my truck. Make sure you put plastic underneath it before you start painting. The brushes are there, too." She points to her truck, parked a few cars down, and encourages them to start soon so that two coats will have time to dry by the time they're finished for the day and have to bring it inside.

Miss Val raises her eyebrows, wiggles her fingers excitedly, and snickers deviously. Everyone giggles nervously.

"Uh oh," Paige says, grinning.

Their teacher disappears inside and comes back out holding some fake grass stalks, smiling mischievously. "These are Wili weeds, as you already know, and after you paint the cross we could staple them to the base. Aren't they cool?" Her weird giggle bubbles up again and her eyes playfully dart around.

The students laugh and roll their eyes knowingly.

"Sure. Whatever you say, Miss Val." Paige takes the Wili weeds from her and holds them upright at the base. "Like this?" She makes the little white stalks dance, and they all crack up again.

"Yes. Just like that. They're perfect." Miss Val motions Todd to come in with the girls to practice Hilarion's death scene with the Wilis. By the end of the dance, Randi and the others are breathing hard, and Todd collapses appropriately onto the floor. Miss Val gives constructive pointers, and then they repeat it with added finesse.

By the end of that Saturday rehearsal, they have practiced and perfected every dance they're involved with in the whole ballet; finished Giselle's cross, except for her name; and rehearsed, fairly successfully, while holding the Wili weeds correctly for the first time. Randi knows how important it is to practice with props far enough ahead of a performance so that it feels second nature. Otherwise the prop can, too easily, be completely forgotten. One time she forgot to carry a basket of flowers on stage and had to pretend it was there. *Not pleasant.* But with enough repetitions, the dancers can solidly rely on muscle memory if they can't consciously remember something. Randi appreciates Miss Val teaching them in so many different ways. She feels lucky to be involved at this studio, with so many good friends. And, to top it off, she's dancing the lead this year! She is becoming Giselle!

10

THE FIELDS' FARM

Deanne

*Sometimes it can be better to just
go with the flow, though not always.
Learn to tell the difference!*

Deanne likes spending time at Brindle's house, where chickens, horses, and goats are more than just yard art. Her friend has the chore of milking goats and then bringing the warm, white liquid inside to filter into jars and deposit into the refrigerator. She has unsuccessfully begged her mom to let her have a goat, but she also realizes suburbia is not the ideal place for keeping livestock. Brindle has shown her how to hold the teat just so, and then gently squeeze from the top downward and aim the stream of milk into the pail. It's not as easy as she thought it would be, but she manages to get a little bit into the bucket.

The Fields' place is out in the sticks at the end of a long dirt road. Miss Val isn't your typical ballet teacher. She has so many interests that don't relate to dance at all, at least as far as Deanne can see. She rides horses, gardens, builds things, runs, and prepares meals for her family using weird things out of the garden like okra, beets, and kale. They eat stuff called "tofu mess" and "wilted chard salad." Deanne prefers normal food like macaroni and cheese or steak and she usually brings her own snacks with her when she comes to visit Brindle.

Last night, she and Brindle had slept in the living room so they could have their own space without Willow. That girl can be a little annoying, like most little sisters are, she assumes. They stayed up late watching *Pride and Prejudice* and slept in; it's a rare Sunday morning that her mom let her off the hook about going to church. After the two of them eat some of the pancakes they'd made, Brindle suggests they play music together. As her friend settles onto the piano bench, she takes her recorder out of the case and begins to blow into it.

"How about some Bach? Do you have music for that?" Deanne asks.

"Of course," Brindle says and opens the bench to pull out a few pages of sheet music. "How about one of these etudes? They're not too difficult."

"Okay." Deanne leans over Brindle's shoulder to read the music. She breathes into her instrument, and the notes from the piano meet hers.

"That sounds beautiful," Miss Val says, passing through the room with a load of laundry.

Deanne nods and hits a wrong note, but keeps playing. Several phrases progress smoothly before Brindle pauses and then rushes to catch up. They both stop.

"Oops, I couldn't get that chord fast enough."

"Let's try again. It wasn't too bad."

This time, they play through the entire piece with only a couple mistakes and give each other high-fives and cheer when they finish.

Six-year-old Taz runs in and jumps onto the couch. "Can I be your audience?"

"Sure. Why not? Is that okay, Deanne?"

"Well, I suppose," she says with a little smile. *He's kind of cute sitting there looking at us like that with his big puppy-dog eyes, through those long blond bangs.*

They play while he listens and applauds for the next ten minutes, until Willow pokes in her head.

"Can I have the rest of the pancakes?"

"Go ahead," Deanne says. "They're probably cold by now."

"Me too!" Taz yells, jumping off the sofa and running after Willow.

The girls put their things away and follow them to the kitchen. Mr. Val is washing garden veggies in the sink.

Miss Val turns off the blender and pours green liquid into a glass. "Would you like to try some, Deanne?"

"Oh, no, thanks. I'm good." *It looks disgusting.*

"Hey, Mom?" Brindle asks. "Do you think Deanne, Sophia, and I could walk to the library on Tuesday?"

"I don't know. How would your mom feel about that, Deanne?"

"I'm sure she'd be fine with it." *I kind of doubt Mother will actually be fine with it, though, and Father will have his say, too, no doubt.*

"I think you and Sophia should talk to your parents about it and then get back to me." Miss Val rinses the blender and heads outside with her smoothie.

Brindle and Deanne decide to take a walk. At least here on the Field's farm, they can go without a chaperone. They wander up the creek bed and find a boulder to sit on.

"You're lucky to live out here, Brindle. It's so beautiful and peaceful. We always have cars zipping right by our house, and at night we hear sirens." But it occurs to her that she only feels this way while she's actually here. Otherwise, she much prefers being around the cooler, older kids in her neighborhood. She's been trying to get in with some high school girls at church. They get to go on dates and have boyfriends.

"I'm sure there are pros and cons. I mean, you like being close to your other friends, right? And being closer to a store if you need something," Brindle says, flicking an ant off her shoe. "I mean, if we run out of something, we don't just drive to the store. Mom makes do with what we have and waits 'til she or Dad is in town anyway."

Deanne drifts into thoughts about boys. "Jack's kind of cute. Don't you think?"

Brindle gives her a quizzical, what-for look. "I suppose."

In the silence that follows, Deanne decides Brindle isn't really the type of friend to discuss this with. She tosses a piece of bark into the creek. A squirrel chirps nearby and she lies back onto the rock, closing her eyes. Before long, she sits up to escape the acorn stabbing her in the back and wonders what time it is.

Brindle tosses a handful of leaves off the boulder, breaking the silence. "Your dancing's gotten so much better this year. Even my mom says so."

"Really? I've been trying extra hard." *That's good that Miss Val's noticed.*

"Maybe it's because you're dancing Randi's parts, too," Brindle says, pulling her knees to her chest and looking at her intently. "You don't actually want Randi *not* to be able to dance the lead, do you?"

"No, of course not. Besides, I haven't done all the partnering moves yet. I wonder what your mom's plans are for that?" She watches a group of baby squirrels running along some nearby rocks. For some reason, it makes her think of how lonely she is sometimes in her own family, compared to what it must be like to have sisters and brothers.

"Hey, does your dad come to *all* your recitals? You know, the music ones, too?"

"Yeah, he does," Brindle answers, tossing an acorn cap into Deanne's lap. "Why do you ask?"

"Just curious. My father hardly ever comes to any of mine. He always says he's too busy." Deanne fidgets with the acorn cap and then breaks it in half. "You're lucky to have a dad like yours. Even if we do all joke around and call him *Mr. Val.*" She smiles at the silly image.

Brindle stares off into the distance as if deep in thought. "But your mom goes to your performances. And I usually do, too."

"I know."

"Mr. Val." Brindle giggles. "It is kind of funny, huh?"

"It's probably because we all know Miss Val and when he's around, he's always helping her."

It's definitely relaxing to hang out with Brindle, who seems happy just being by herself so much of the time. The two of them are so different from each other. Brindle is kind of a loner, except for Sophia. And she likes talking with adults. She doesn't really have any other friends. *Maybe that's why I'm her friend.* She doesn't know anyone else quite like Brindle and so it's sort of interesting to have her for a friend, too. At least they have dance in common and can play music together. And there are the books.

The girls walk back by the garden and find Miss Val kneeling in the dirt. She pulls up a carrot and puts it in a basket full of green edibles.

"Did you two have a nice walk? It sure is a lovely day, isn't it?"

"Yes it is," Deanne answers, looking around at all the salad greens growing around her. "Do you guys actually eat all this?" *There's so much.*

Miss Val dusts off her hands and stands up. Her blonde hair falls around her shoulders under a floppy straw hat. "Mm hmm. Well, mostly. We give some of it away."

Mr. Val makes his way up the hill toward them pushing a wheelbarrow full of horse manure and dumps it on the compost heap. "Are you picking our dinner, Val?"

"You bet," she says, closing the garden gate before heading back to the house with the girls. "What time is your mom picking you up, Deanne?"

"I think pretty soon. I better go pack."

The phone is ringing when they reach the house, and Miss Val hurries in the door to answer it. They still have a landline out here since cell reception is spotty. Deanne hears her talking about the backdrop for the ballet and something about looking forward to seeing it on Tuesday.

After Miss Val hangs up, Deanne asks, "Will the backdrop be coming to the studio? I can't wait to see it."

"It's the night scene at the lake, right, Mom?" Brindle asks, closing the kitchen door behind her.

"Yes to both your questions. I hope it turns out like what we want."

Deanne's mom arrives to pick her up. On the drive home, she asks Deanne the usual questions like what they did, if she had fun, etc. After assuring her mother that, yes, she had indeed enjoyed herself, she closes her eyes. Ah, nothing like a day in the country with her friend, even if they don't agree on the whole women's march thing. They had decided to bench that topic for a while.

At last, Deanne's wishes have come true, and by the next weekend she has a new group of really cool friends from her church youth group. They are in high school and have boyfriends, at least they say they do. She told them she was in high school, too. *I will be by next year*

anyway. And they have actually begun to include her in their conversations.

But now Deanne lies on her bed fuming about her parents. *How could they? How dare they?* She finally got in with these new older kids—AT CHURCH—and they invited her to go with them to see the latest Marvel movie. Getting accepted by these fun, popular girls is very important to her. Can't her parents see that? And now they won't let her go. They say it's not appropriate for her age. Actually, it was her father who said that, and of course, he always has the last say. *Come to think of it, he has all the "says" in our house. What a tyrant.* How is she supposed to grow up normal when her parents won't let her do anything? *I'll still be stunted at thirteen when I'm twenty-five.* Deanne rolls over and screams into her pillow, eventually crying herself to sleep.

Deanne's favorite song plays on her iPod and the heavy base reverberates through the house. She twirls and shimmies while putting on her torso-hugging top and new skinny jeans. She sings along loudly, "Whatcha gonna give me?" while buckling the straps of the high-wedge sandals she'd secretly bought at the mall. She is pumped up and can't wait to go. The song changes and she anxiously drums her fingers on the table and bobs her head impatiently. *What's taking them so long?* The clock in the living room chimes four times and she re-reads the note she's written.

Dear Mother,
I'm studying at the library with
Brindle and will call you later.
Love, Deanne

Finally, the doorbell rings. Deanne grabs her coat, takes one last look around at the sparkling clean kitchen she's leaving behind, and goes out the door. Hurrying down the walkway with the heavily made-up blonde girl, she catches sight of the neighbor watering his yard. *Uh oh. I hope he doesn't rat me out.* She smiles and waves at him, hoping to look natural, and quickly slides into the back seat, making three across.

"How'd you get away?" the driver asks, who happens to be a guy!

Oh boy, I sure hope I don't get caught. I could get in SO much trouble.

Deanne can see his riveting brown eyes looking back at her in the rear-view mirror.

"Uh." *Pull it together now.* "I have my ways."

"Okay then," he says and the five of them cackle like a clutch of hens, except for the throaty laugh of the driver. The car screeches away from the curb and heads to the forbidden movie.

Almost immediately, the two in the front seat start kissing. The car wobbles and Deanne squirms uncomfortably. The girl next to her lights up a cigarette and offers her one.

These are *church* kids. *Why are they behaving like this?* "No thanks."

Trees and houses whiz by the side windows as the car speeds haphazardly down the street. The driver spins a donut in the parking lot before crookedly pulling into a space. As they get out of the car, Deanne takes a deep breath and tries to calm herself. *I am going to be in SO much trouble.*

They purchase their tickets at the outside window and make their way into the theater. Deanne excuses herself to the restroom and passes the flashing lights of the concession counter. The smell of hot, buttery popcorn hangs in the stagnant air. Unfortunately, the other girls join her, giggling uncontrollably. *Are they high?*

Deanne quickly closes the door of the bathroom stall and stands there, her heart pounding. *I can't go through with this. I am SO out of my league here. How am I going to get out of this?* She wracks her brain unsuccessfully, too upset to think. *Please, God, help me figure this out.*

She flushes the toilet, so the girls won't get suspicious, and then, finally, an idea comes to her. Not a very good one, but perhaps one that won't get her in *quite* as much trouble. Deanne goes out to wash her hands and confides to the one girl still waiting for her in the restroom.

"I'm not feeling very well. You guys go ahead without me. I'll find a ride home on my own. I'm so sorry."

"Okay. No worries," the girl says. "Hope you feel better." She wiggles her fingers over her shoulder in a cursory wave, without even looking back.

Deanne takes a few minutes to compose herself before going outside to call her mother. She steals herself for the absolutely terrifying repercussions sure to come.

11

THE FIRST FULL REHEARSAL

Randi

*Don't forget to use the feet when
pushing off for a jump.*

"I can't believe we're already in full rehearsals," Paige says, tying her *pointe* shoe ribbons around her ankles.

"Well, it is mid-May. It's time, don't you think?" Annie says, grabbing her heel from a sitting position and straightening her long, lean leg upward.

"Just saying." Paige stands up and leans into her *pointe*, arching her right shoe. "Time's flying, and I can hardly believe that Randi and I will already be juniors next year."

Randi sits in her splits, adjusting her weight one way and then the other, stretching her hamstrings. They're a little tighter than usual. *Probably because of that plastique class yesterday.* Miss Val had really put them through the wringer with a whole hour of nothing but stretching. But it's a good kind of pain. "Well, I, for one, will be glad when my English and math classes are over. I'm ready for a break."

"But," Paige says. "That means our performances would be over, too."

"That's true," Randi says. "I don't want to rush that. I am excited that we're in full rehearsals now. This is when it all starts coming together."

Randi tries to hide her insecurities. She has all the dances memorized now, but every time she dances with Jack, she falls apart. She tries the whole "letting go thing" again, but that just makes it worse. She needs a new tactic.

"All right," Miss Val says, walking over to the group. "So, as you know from previous years, we will spend most of this Advanced class time on the pieces the other groups are not a part of. And we'll run through the others a little as well. In an hour-and-a-half, the Beginning and Intermediate classes will join us to work on the group dances and then we'll do a complete run-through if there's time."

"We have four full rehearsals here before the dress rehearsal on the stage, right?" Randi asks, changing her splits to the other side.

"Yes, that's correct. It's usually a bit chaotic for this first run-through, and I need you all to be patient with the multiple repetitions we'll have to do with the little kids."

"Of course we will," Annie says. "They're so cute." She gets up and opens the glass door, letting the warm spring air enter the studio.

"Thank you, Annie," Miss Val says. "One of the reasons we do these full rehearsals is to get the young ones acquainted to being on stage with you older students, and used to dancing in front of an audience. And they get to watch the duets and other pieces they're not in. Okay?"

"Yes, ma'am," Todd spouts, with overdone enthusiasm.

Paige, in a good-natured gesture, throws a ballet slipper at him.

"I'm mortally wounded," Todd whines, rolling to his back and putting his arms and legs up in the air, playing dead.

"Again? Really?" Paige rolls her eyes teasingly.

"All right then. Let the fun begin." Miss Val walks over to the stereo, holding her notepad.

They do a short *barre* before running through their dances. When it's time to practice their first duet, Randi figures it's time to go back to her original plan. Instead of getting all flustered and embarrassed, she'll try concentrating really hard on herself. Just her. And do her very best. No more of that "letting go" thing. She can, at least, attempt to be responsible for herself. Once again.

Todd and Miss Val carry a mat from behind the curtain and unfold it in the middle of the floor. Randi looks at herself in the mirror and steps onto the middle panel while Jack stands on the one behind. Todd takes his position directly behind Jack, while Miss Val, Paige, and Annie complete the spotting circle around them.

"On three," Miss Val says. "Is everyone ready? And Randi, remember to push through your feet in the jump."

Randi nods nervously. *I hate this stunt. It's way too scary.*

Everyone else affirms, ready to spot if needed, and Miss Val counts to three. Randi jumps, Jack lifts, and the other four bend their knees and lift their arms in readiness. Randi makes it as far as Jack's chest and then slides down the front of his body.

Okay. Just picture being perched up on his shoulder. I can do this. She forces her feelings aside and makes it happen. She jumps strongly, pushes out her butt, and slides onto his shoulder. *It works!*

Jack turns around with a bounce, making her dizzy.

"I knew you guys could do it!" Paige claps.

"Well done," Miss Val says. "Okay, Deanne. Your turn."

"Really?" Deanne shrieks. "Okay then!" She bounds over to the mat and takes Randi's place.

After only three tries, the younger girl makes it up onto Jack's shoulder and throws her arms up in the air.

How can she be so fearless? Randi watches as the two of them perform it twice more and then practice the spotted *pirouettes. It's not fair. She's two years younger than me and is so precise in her movements.* Randi is more enthralled with the grace and flowing nature of ballet, while Deanne seems better at linking steps together.

"Your dancing is more graceful than hers," Paige whispers.

Did she just read my mind? "Thanks, but she nailed it."

Wind gusts in the open door, sending Randi's ballet skirt upward, giving her a chance to wipe her sweaty hands as she adjusts it back down. As the afternoon progresses, they rehearse their duets and she finds her new plan is actually working. Sometimes. *Better than no plan.* At least it gives her something else to think about, just herself, instead of Jack's warm hands on her body and their proximity to each other. *Just turn off those feelings.*

After their Advanced class, the others walk outside for a ten-minute break when the younger students arrive to start their warm-up. Randi stays in to help Miss Val. One of the newer little girls doesn't want to come in since more people than usual are practicing in the studio, but Miss Val coaxes her into joining with some encouraging words. Their teacher definitely has a way with kids. Randi had already tried without success.

Before the main characters come back in, she and Miss Val go over the village dances with the younger students. Then, when they're all together, Miss Val counts out the phrasing of the village scene and leads the entire Act I cast through their steps. She always does this before they dance with the music. Randi knows she wants to make sure everyone is clear on where they have to be and what steps they are supposed to do while she can stop and re-teach if necessary. Finally, Randi thinks, they're all going to dance to the music together for the very first time.

"Places, everyone! Ready?" The music begins. "Smile, you guys. Look like you're having fun. This is supposed to be a happy, festive celebration!"

The Advanced girls skip around the stage, partnering with the younger ones from time to time, keeping the flow of the dance going with the creative choreography. When Randi and Jack dance together, the little girls can't help but stop and watch with their mouths hanging open, entranced. Miss Val reminds them that they, too, are on stage and have to look like villagers in the scene.

They run through Act One again before Miss Val says, "How would you guys like to be the audience now and watch the dance of the Wilis?"

"Yay!" The Beginners jump up and down excitedly before sitting in front, legs crossed tightly, backs against the mirrors.

The Intermediate students are Wilis and go to their places. Again, as before, Miss Val prompts them through the movements without music, ironing out a few glitches as they arise. When the group finally performs it with music, complete with Hilarion's demise and Albrecht's broken heart, the Beginners sit transfixed. Randi still thinks they're cute, even if they are a pain sometimes. When it ends, Miss Val leads them into applause.

"Let's see it again!" one little girl shouts.

"Okay, but after we fix a few things."

Randi watches Lisa, the heavyset girl with a bad attitude, roll her eyes when Willow endures a brief scolding from her mother for goofing around.

"What's your problem?" asks the girl with a perfect little ballerina body.

"None of your business," Lisa says, moving away from her.

"What's up, anyway?" Randi asks. She'll see if she can handle this like a teacher would.

"She's such a know-it-all. That's all."

"Well, try not to let it get to you. This rehearsal is fun, isn't it?" *Changing the subject might work.*

She smiles slightly. "Yeah, I guess so."

While Miss Val works with the Intermediate group, Randi stretches near the three middle school girls.

"It's too bad we didn't get to walk to the library. How come your mom said no, anyway?" Sophia asks.

Deanne looks around. "I'm grounded." The poor girl looks crestfallen.

"Why? What happened?" Brindle asks.

Randi elbows Paige. "Hey," she whispers. "We gotta hear this."

"I snuck out to a movie with some friends from church."

Her two friends look shocked.

Randi whispers, "She probably thinks she's so grown up and cool," then rolls her eyes.

"Maybe not so cool?" Paige says quietly.

"Thanks a lot, Deanne," Brindle says, obviously annoyed. "Didn't you think that might ruin it for the rest of us? I mean, about getting to walk to the library by ourselves between classes. You should've told us."

"Pretty pathetic. The library, really? Not a big deal." Deanne sneers.

"It is when *WE* don't get to do it because of *YOU*!" Sophia huffs and goes over to get her water bottle out of her ballet bag.

Brindle gives Deanne the evil eye.

"You guys have no clue!" Deanne hisses.

Randi watches Deanne's eyes pool with tears.

"My parents took away my toe shoes for a month! I'm going to get so weak! I can only dance in my ballet slippers."

"Man, that's harsh," Paige says.

"Yeah. That's too bad. I don't know how I'd handle that if it happened to me." Randi thinks for a moment and braces herself before going over to comfort Deanne. She doesn't want to, but, "Rise above, right?"

"Mm hmm," Paige answers.

Randi sits down next to her. "Hey, Deanne? I'm sure you'll keep your strength." She does feel sorry for her and remembers how hard it was when she was one of the younger kids in the Advanced class, trying to figure out where she fit into the already existing pecking order.

Deanne wipes her eyes and straightens up, softening a little to Randi's gesture. "No, I won't." Then she excuses herself and heads to the bathroom.

Annie comes over to Randi. "What was that about?"

"Deanne drama," Randi says.

"Huh? Oh," Annie acknowledges.

Randi smiles as if a weight has been lifted from her. *Maybe Deanne will stop trying so hard to be better than me.*

"Hey, Randi? Do you have any nail clippers in your bag?" Annie asks.

"Sure, I'll get them." She wanders over to her bag, trying to make sense of what just happened, but comes up with nothing. "Here you go, Annie."

The dancers are constantly fussing with their toenails since they wear *pointe* shoes. If they get too long, the pressure can make them hurt and even get infected. But still, Randi believes the pros far outweigh the cons. *Pointe* work is so beautiful.

One of the Intermediate students follows Randi and Annie over to the corner to watch. Anything about dancing *en pointe* seems to interest her. "How long have you had toe shoes, Annie?"

"Three years. It's a lot harder than it looks. How old are you?"

"I just turned eleven." She stares at the shiny pink shoes.

"Who knows?" Annie says. "Sometimes Miss Val will let students get *pointe* shoes before they're thirteen. If they're ready."

Annie hands the clippers back and Randi asks, "Would you like to feel them?"

The young ballerina kneels down and runs her fingers along the box of the shoe and stops at the toe. "Why is it so scuffed up here?"

Randi lifts her heels and rises to *elevé*. "Because, that's the part we dance on. See?"

The cast practices Act Two one more time before Miss Val excuses them and stands in the doorway to make sure no little kids escape without a parent. A man squeezes in carrying an armload of heavy canvas.

Brindle pokes Deanne on the shoulder. "I bet that's the backdrop!"

Deanne leans away, but says, "Can we see it?"

Randi watches Deanne follow Brindle and Sophia to the center of the room and joins them.

"Sure. Can you help me unfold it?" The wiry little man drops the canvas.

The five of them carefully lay out the large tapestry on the studio floor, following the man's lead.

"Wow. It's gorgeous!" Miss Val exclaims, walking around the edges and admiring the details. The shimmering lake looks almost real.

"Is it what you wanted?" he asks, smiling up at her from his kneeling position.

"Well, yes. And more. You've really outdone yourself. Is our trade for your daughter's classes going to be enough for this?"

"You bet." He winks and says, "She gets so much out of her classes here." He scans the room, glancing at his daughter outside. "Her confidence has improved immensely, too. I'm happy to do it."

"What do you think, girls?"

"It's awesome," Brindle says.

Randi says, "I can't believe how well it turned out. It must be great to be an artist."

"Well, you're all artists too, you know," he says.

Miss Val affirms his statement and helps refold the backdrop and stuff it into a large trash bag. She puts a strip of duct tape on the black plastic and labels it *Lake Backdrop*. It's been a productive afternoon at the ballet studio, and Randi feels relieved when she finally sees her mom pull up outside. The exhaustion of concentrating so hard on herself, to push away those uncomfortable feelings she gets when she's around Jack, has caught up with her and she can't wait to get home and relax. *Are things really beginning to fall into place?*

12

A Trip to the Mall

Randi

*Keep a joyful face—you never know
when a snapshot might be taken.*

Randi is already on her last good pair of ballet
pink tights and still has several more rehearsals
and classes, plus the dress rehearsal and
performances, to get through. She talks Paige into
joining her on a trip to the mall, which isn't all that
difficult. Her mom offers to take them that Sunday in
the middle of May, since she has business to attend to
down in San Diego.

"It's nice to get out of Nuevo once in a while," Paige
says, absently pointing out their reflections in the shop
windows as they walk by.

"I know it, huh? I like to get down the hill at
least every couple weeks. Nuevo can be a little small-
townish." Randi stops to check out a cute pair of
shoes on display before walking toward the escalator.

Upstairs, huge skylights let in massive amounts of bright light, creating a cheery atmosphere.

The dancewear shop has little girl mannequins in the window wearing cute green and pink tutus. Randi goes in and rifles through the tights in her size.

Paige stands in front of the *pointe* shoes and calls for Randi to come over. "Aren't these the same brand Bree used to wear?"

Randi looks at the box underneath the shoe. "Yeah, I think so." She puts the box back in place and pauses, looking at all the beautiful, unblemished *pointe* shoes. *They're so pretty when they're new.* "I miss having Bree in class. I didn't know her all that well, but still." She runs her fingers along the smooth vamp of the shoe, caressing the soft, pink satin. "Don't get me wrong. I'm super thrilled to dance the lead, but it's a little scary being the one who's not supposed to mess up. I liked being able to follow her."

"She was a beautiful dancer, wasn't she?" Paige takes the shoe from her and puts it back. "It must feel kind of weird sometimes, when the whole cast looks up to you."

"Oh, my gosh, Paige. Now you're making me feel a little freaked out. Too much pressure." Randi scoffs and goes back to the tights. She buys two pairs, planning to wear her old ones for the rest of the rehearsals and save the new ones for the performances.

The two girls wander through the food court and happen upon their ballet classmates, the three middle schoolers, eating lunch at a table across the floor.

"Whoa. What are the chances of that?" Randi asks.

Paige puts her index finger to her lips, then ushers Randi the long way around to go up behind them. They manage to get close enough to overhear their conversation.

"Honestly, I think I could do the part better than Randi. Haven't you guys seen how she keeps messing up?" Deanne takes a sip of her drink and shrugs her shoulders. "Well?"

"Sure. She does, sometimes. But I think she's a beautiful dancer," Sophia says, shaking her head at the understudy.

"We all know how much you'd love to be Giselle, but it *is* Randi's turn. Just let her enjoy it, okay?" Brindle turns around in time to see Paige grab a French fry off Deanne's plate.

Randi forces a fake smile, pretending she hasn't heard their discussion. *Too late to back away now.*

Deanne turns around and shrieks. "Oh my gosh! What are you guys doing here?"

Paige steps back. "Picking up some tights and hanging out. What about you? I thought you were grounded."

"I am, sort of. But the main thing is that I'm not allowed to get my toe shoes back until *after* our concert." She pouts. "Which really sucks."

Sophia and Brindle giggle when Paige swipes another fry from Deanne's plate.

"Hey, thief!" Deanne scolds.

"Who brought you guys?" Paige asks.

Randi's a little too hurt to join in.

"My mom did," Deanne responds. "She had some shopping to do here."

"This is so much fun!" Sophia giggles. "I mean, seeing you guys here like this."

"Interesting, huh?" Well, we gotta go. See you at ballet." Paige grabs Randi's arm and ushers her away.

As they leave the food court, Randi looks back at the three musketeers huddled together and wonders if Deanne feels any guilt whatsoever for what she had to have known they'd overheard.

"Deanne clearly doesn't like me. And she thinks I'm a horrible dancer."

"I'm sorry you had to hear her talk that way about you. But it's not true, anyway. So, don't worry about it."

"Easy for you to say. They weren't talking about *you*," Randi says.

"Well, anyway, they were clearly excited to be alone in the mall without supervision, weren't they? Remember how fun it was when we were that age, getting to explore the mall all by ourselves for the first time?" Paige asks.

"Of course, I do."

"I remember being absolutely twitterpated." Paige drums her fingers on her chest, feigning excitement.

Randi's mood improves and they laugh and ride the escalator back downstairs to go to one of the department stores to try on cute summer dresses. Nana had given her birthday money for a new outfit. Walking through the men's section, Paige pulls a pair of board shorts from the rack.

"Hey, don't these look like something Jack would wear?" Paige works her eyebrows up and down for emphasis.

"What are you doing? Is there something wrong with your eyebrows, Paige?"

"I know you like Jack," Paige teases. "I've seen you checking him out."

"Well, I was probably just tired and didn't realize where my eyes were resting," Randi says, walking away toward the teen section. *Sometimes Paige can be a little nosy.*

"Oh, no you don't. You can't tell me that you don't like him. Just a little. Can you?"

"Well," Randi stops. "I don't *not* like him. But I don't like him the way you're talking about." She giggles and turns away with a smile. Why does her friend always have to be so perceptive, anyway? "Don't go so *Paige* on me. Honestly."

"I knew it." Paige laughs and hurries to catch up. Thankfully, she lets the topic drop—for now.

Randi holds up a small, yellow, spaghetti-strapped dress. "This one's kinda cute, don't you think?"

"Ooh, I like it. You should try it on." Paige rummages through the next rack.

"Okay, I will. But first, you find something to try on, too."

Paige pushes things from right to left until she finds an orange, flowered sundress. They hurry to the dressing rooms.

"Do you think this looks okay or does it make me look fat?" Paige asks, opening the curtain so her friend can see.

"No, Paige, it doesn't. And you are *not* fat." Randi knows her friend would like to lose a few pounds, but she enjoys food too much. "Let's see. Turn around."

Paige twirls around, letting the skirt flare around her.

"It's cute. I like it. Do you?"

"Yes. And I like yours, too. We should get them," Paige says.

"Okay!" Randi giggles and they bump knuckles, wiggle their fingers, and say in unison, "Phew," before retreating to their little curtained-off rooms.

After making their purchases, Paige says, "I want to wear mine now."

Randi agrees, so they find a bathroom and change into their pretty new dresses. They decide ice cream is next on the agenda and make their way to the other end of the mall.

"Are you nervous about getting your driver's license?" Paige asks, weaving her way through the crowd.

"Sort of. David says it's no big deal though."

"Of course your brother would say that. Nothing's a big deal to him. He's Mister Man on Campus. He's not scared of anything."

The girls laugh and continue making their way through the throngs of shoppers.

"What's he want to be when he grows up, anyway?" Paige always asks questions like this, out of the blue.

Randi ponders. "Who knows?" She shakes her head and tries to imagine her brother all grown up. She can't really. "Maybe a professional soccer player or some lame thing."

"It's not that lame. He probably could, you know, if that's what he wants. Anyway, I think I'm waiting until summer to get my learner's permit. I need to focus on finals and our performances," Paige says.

"I feel like I need as much practice as possible. Oh, you know what? My mom just told us we're going to Arizona next week for a relative's wedding. Maybe I could drive part of the way there."

"Really? How long are you going to be gone for?" Paige asks, smiling at their reflection as they walk by a window.

Randi nods. "Only for a long weekend. Don't worry, I won't miss any Tuesday rehearsals. Miss Val would kill me."

"Speaking of Miss Val, she's gotta be worried about Todd's ankle. He's been hobbling around for weeks," Paige says, speeding up to get around a stroller.

"But I bet she's glad it didn't happen at the studio. Didn't he jump over a fence or something at school?"

"Yeah, I think so. The moron," Paige says jokingly. "He's such a goof off."

"Well, I sure hope it heals quickly. He's doing so well as Hilarion, even so."

They settle into a booth and order ice cream sundaes. Randi takes too many bites in rapid succession and gets an immediate ice cream headache. She squeezes her eyes shut and puts a fist on her forehead.

"Oh, I'm sorry," Paige says, patting her hand on the table. "Pace yourself."

Randi takes a deep breath and pushes her bowl to the center of the table. "I think I need to slow down."

Three guys walk by and one of them points to Randi. "Brain freeze?"

Randi nods and he leaves with his friends saying, "Too bad, so sad."

The girls wave. When the boys are out of sight, Paige grins. "The one without the cap was cute, huh?"

"Sort of," Randi says, getting back to eating her ice cream, a bit more cautiously now.

Later, when Randi opens her closet to put away her new purchases, she notices the Christmas card from her grandmother. She'd kept the beautiful picture of the wild coyote on the front of the card visible so she sees it every time she opens the door. Feeling a little tug on the heartstrings, she decides to call her.

"Hey, Coyote. What's new?"

Randi gives a little yip, talks about the wedding in Arizona, and says she wishes Nana could go with them.

"Yeah, me too. But don't worry. I'll see you at your big performance. How are rehearsals coming along?"

"Okay, I guess. I'm getting a little better. But that girl, Deanne, is still trying to get my part—*and* she's my understudy."

"What? How's that?"

"Well, she dances behind me, learning my steps. And actually, she's really good at it. I'm a little worried, Nana." Randi appreciates being able to confide in her grandmother.

"Has your teacher said anything? You know, about replacing you?" Nana always gets to the point.

"Well, no, but I'm still having a hard time with it. That girl's seriously undermining me."

"Now look here, Randi. Get her out of your head right now. Just buck up and do your best. Don't let your fears ruin this wonderful opportunity you have to dance the part of Giselle!"

Randi knows in her heart that Nana's right, as usual. They talk for a half hour before her grandma says it's time to feed her cats, and they end their conversation. She remembers her new shoes, takes the box from the closet, and pulls open the crinkly white tissue inside—revealing her shiny, pink *pointe* shoes. She leans forward, breathing in their enticing, not-yet-worn smell and smiles. *Non-dancers don't know what they're missing.* After neatly setting them side by side on the bed next to her, she unfolds the supple satin ribbon before refolding it to cut in half, and then each in half again. The grey tabby jumps up to join her.

"Not now, Butch. I'm busy." She edges him off her pillow and he meows loudly in protest before leaving the room.

Taking an end of one of the ribbons, she folds the tip back on itself and hems it into the shoe, stitching the familiar box pattern before finishing on the diagonal. She repeats the process three more times before tackling the elastics. These will be fastened nearer the heel to keep the shoes from slipping off.

As Randi completes her task, evening light yellows her room from the west-facing window. She turns to lie on her stomach and watches the last rays of the sun filter through the leaves of the towering eucalyptus tree in the backyard. Arching upward, she stretches her back and gazes out, inhaling the fresh air into her lungs. The breeze gently ripples the open curtain and a few fraying threads dance erratically.

Butch returns, announcing himself annoyingly, before leaping up and knocking the sewing supplies onto the floor.

"Butch!" Randi quickly shoos him off the bed and looks for the needle in the pile below. "Where is it?"

She wraps the newly sewn-on ribbons around each shoe and gently places them back into the box. Without thinking, she pushes herself off the bed and immediately feels a sharp stab of pain go up her heel.

"Ouch!" she screams.

The cat bolts out of the room.

"Holy cats! What the heck?"

The words come ripping out before she can stop them. She tentatively hops on one foot, back to the bed, and sits down to analyze her injury. *There's nothing there. Why does it hurt so much?* She pushes gently into her heel and feels another rush of pain. *There's something hard in there.* She carefully feels around some more.

"Mom? Mom! Could you come in here?" She's shaking.

"I'm coming!"

Randi wipes tears from her eyes when Mom steps into the open doorway.

"What's wrong?"

Randi whimpers, "I think my sewing needle went all the way into my heel." She sniffles and stares at the bottom of her foot, about ready to faint. "It's completely in there, I think. I can't even see it." She feels sick.

Mom sits down beside her and cradles the injured foot in her hands. Gently turning it this way and that, she looks perplexed.

Randi's stomach churns and her mind races. "What if I can't dance?" Her voice trembles.

"We better get you to the doctor. David!"

When her brother comes in, Mom explains what happened and has him help get Randi out to the car. Leaning on both their shoulders, she hops along slowly, making sure not to put any weight on her right foot. The car ride is a blur while she struggles not to throw up.

The bright lights of the exam room hurt her eyes and a sharp whiff of rubbing alcohol makes Randi swallow hard and try, unsuccessfully, not to worry. The doctor leans over, palpates the bottom of her heel, and shakes his balding head.

"Well, I'll be darned. That devil went all the way in there, didn't it?" He looks up at her from his rolling stool and grins. "No worries. I can get it out for ya."

"I sure hope so. I'm a dancer and I need to be able to dance *en pointe*," Randi belts out. "I'm dancing the lead in *Giselle*."

"Is that right?" He looks at her mother.

"Well, yes," Mom says, smiling at her. "Will she be able to dance again soon?"

I'm glad she's asking these questions.

"Well, let's check it out first. Shall we?" He leans his head out the door and signals a nurse to come in.

Randi feels her world shrinking as stainless steel instruments are unwrapped and placed on a tray while voices muffle and become indistinct. Time unfolds in a slow blur of activity around her foot, with periodic moments of piercing pain. She braces herself and wills it to be over soon. Finally it is.

The doctor asks her to attempt walking lightly on that foot. She tries, but it's painful. An hour later, an x-ray reveals the small point of the needle embedded in her heel bone.

This time Randi tastes vomit, but steels herself.

"Believe it or not, the best thing to do is leave it in there," the doctor says. His grey mustache twitches as he talks.

"You're kidding," Randi says. "Aren't you?"

He smiles and reaches into his white coat pocket. "Nope, I'm not." He pulls out a green lollypop and hands it to her. "For the trooper. Or rather, the dancer."

Does he think I'm five-years-old or something? She takes the sucker anyway.

On the way home, Randi begs her mom not to tell Miss Val about the tip of the needle being embedded in her heel bone. "In fact, don't tell anyone! Agreed? I lucked out getting this part, and I don't want anything to mess it up. Okay?"

"For now," Mom says.

Randi's thoughts race out of control. *What if it stays too painful to wear my pointe shoes? What if the needle works its way out of the bone and drifts through my bloodstream and gives me a heart attack or something?*

Mom assures her that the doctor had told her she should be fine. "Just a little tender at first. You've got a long weekend ahead of you to recover." She reaches over and pats her knee encouragingly.

Randi stares out the window at a bright, moonlit field filled with sawed-off tree stumps. The image gets her thinking about sawed-off legs and she worries about the possibility of her own leg needing to be amputated because of some out-of-control infection spreading from a germy needle. *What if I can never dance again?*

13

GYMNASTICS FULL REHEARSAL

Deanne

Dance for the sheer joy of it!

Miss Val pulls into the lot in front of the studio after picking up the girls at school. Willow runs to the sidewalk and Deanne stares at the white blinds hanging down behind the two large front windows, which makes the pink stenciled dancer and *Dance Centre* stand out.

"Hey, Mom?" Brindle asks. "Did you bring the sandwiches for dinner?"

Miss Val answers, "Yes, they're in the ice chest. Let's leave them in the car and eat on the way to the movie tonight."

Deanne's club sandwich supper is still in her backpack from this morning. She's looking forward to Thursday family night at the cinema, when a ticket and popcorn are seven dollars. Luckily, Brindle has forgiven her for being the reason they can't walk to the library from the studio by themselves. She's still semi-grounded, but her parents are at least allowing her to go out with Miss Val's family since they seem to value her influence. Brindle never seems to harbor a grudge for long and Deanne's grateful for that. It may not be the same thrilling kind of adventure she had at the movies last time, but this suits her just fine for now. And today she gets to watch the Thursday gymnastics classes *and* go to a movie. They usually do this every couple months or whenever there's a good movie playing.

She and Brindle settle in the storage area behind the back curtain and start reading while Willow does homework. She knows they have to be quiet and not disturb the classes. The pre-school tumbling class is first and Deanne catches glimpses of their little bodies as they pass by the small opening in the drape.

"Okay, you guys. Let's bridge up now," Miss Val instructs. She moves from student to student and gently lifts their hips toward the ceiling. Only one of them arches up all the way by herself, pushing her head off the mat. Later, they somersault and turn baby cartwheels.

Miss Val laughs when one of them squeals, "I love doing cartonwheels!"

She giggles, too. "Hey, did you get number four on the math assignment?" Deanne decides she'd better finish her homework now, since she won't have time later.

Brindle pulls the heavy book out of her backpack and opens it to the page where her math paper sticks out. "I think it's 2,415. What did you get?"

"Oh good. That's what I got, too. I just wanted to make sure I was using the right formula."

"Yeah, sometimes those story problems can be confusing," Brindle says.

Just then, two little gymnasts pass by the back curtain on the way to their tumbling lines.

"You're a fishgut," one of them says.

Both Deanne's and Brindle's jaws drop.

Miss Val says, "Excuse me?" and then asks JP to take over. "Come with me. Now."

Miss Val and the little potty-mouth come back behind the curtain. "What did you call her?" the teacher asks.

The poor little girl looks up with big brown eyes and repeats, "fishgut." She doesn't even look like she knows she did something wrong.

Miss Val takes a deep breath and looks at Deanne and Brindle, as if to gather her thoughts. "And why would you say something like that? It's not very nice, you know."

She stares at the older girls before looking up at her teacher. "I just wanted to see what fish and gut sound like together. That's all."

Miss Val looks about ready to crack up, but makes her tone serious. "Well, that's an interesting demonstration of a compound word, but you really can't say mean things here in the studio. Or at school. We need to try to be nice to everyone and not say hurtful words, even if they sound interesting. Do you understand?"

The girl nods solemnly.

"Okay then. When we go back out there, I want you to apologize very quietly when you're waiting in your line. Deal?"

She nods again, and Miss Val leads her out, shaking her head and rolling her eyes. After they disappear, the older girls can't help giggling.

"Girls?" Miss Val wiggles the curtain in front of them, making them stop.

Deanne whispers, "I thought she actually said something else. I would've got a spanking if I ever talked like that. She must not have very good parents is all I can say."

Brindle, evidently, doesn't want to continue in this vein and changes the subject. "What are you writing your book report on for English?"

Recognizing the topic must be closed, Deanne answers, "*Pride and Prejudice,* of course. What'd you expect?"

Brindle gives her a little push. "Me too." She shakes her head. "Of course."

The girls laugh again and Willow turns around and glares at them. "I'm gonna go change." She picks up her bag and heads to the bathroom. Her class is after the Intermediate gymnastics.

"I wish my mom would let me take gymnastics. She thinks I'm busy enough as it is, though," Deanne says.

Brindle puts the math book back into her backpack. "I used to do it, remember? But I haven't since sixth grade. I like ballet better. Besides, Willow was always better at it than me, and she's three years younger."

"At least you have a little sister," Deanne says, doodling in her notebook.

"You can have her if you want," Brindle teases, raising her dark eyebrows inquiringly. "She's kind of a pain, you know."

"Yeah. She is, sort of, huh? But still."

"I know. But she's okay sometimes." Brindle takes her hair out of the scrunchie and shakes her head from side to side, letting her long blonde hair relax before tying it back up again.

Willow returns wearing black bike shorts and an orange tank top. She has her hair in a short ponytail. Later, the Advanced gymnasts come in.

Willow greets her tomboy friend. "You're still coming to the movie with us after class, right?"

"Yup," she says and then runs across the mat finishing with a roundoff.

"Not 'til after warm-ups!" Miss Val calls, wagging her finger and shaking her head. "JP! Can you start warm-ups, please?"

The students stand on the mats, feet apart, facing the mirror, and circle their arms backward following Miss Val's assistant. Deanne watches them lean into backbends and then hold their right leg straight up, then change to the left, and do the same with their arms. Their tumbling runs are spectacular: roundoffs, back handsprings, walking on their hands, back-walkovers, front and back flips, and aerials. Then they rehearse the hunter piece for *Giselle*.

Willow passes out the bows—no arrows—to everyone. These are bent sticks with a string tied onto each end. When the music begins, they lunge onto the mats, pointing their bows at one another before continuing as a group. Deanne can't help but laugh. She figures the beginning is meant to be humorous, but with half of them messing up it's even funnier. One guy's string breaks and it dangles limply from the bottom of his little bow. He pouts for effect and then ditches it off to the side of the mat. She notices Miss Val smile and roll her eyes when the tomboy's bow snaps in half and falls on the floor.

"What a disaster!" Miss Val teases above the music. "Don't pull so hard on the strings, you guys. These have to last a while, you know."

The music picks up, and the gymnasts begin doing stunts, some of them still holding props and others not. Willow takes off across the diagonal, performing a roundoff, back handspring, back tuck—all the while clutching her weapon. Deanne is both impressed and envious. She wishes she could do that. It looks like fun. At the end, the hunters exit, stage right.

Miss Val calls them all back to sit down and stretch on the mats. "Not too bad. But, not that great, either. You two need to be sharper on your executions. And you," she says pointing at Willow's friend. "What are those things attached to the ends of your legs?"

"Feet?" she asks.

"Yes. And what are you supposed to do with them?"

"Point them?"

"Yes, indeed. You all must remember to point your toes. You may be hunters, but you have to look sharp!"

JP calls out, "Where's Willow? Oh, there you are. Tighten your center, okay?"

Willow nods and cracks her neck while the corrections continue.

They run through the piece a couple more times. Before Deanne knows it, class is over and it's almost time to go to the movie. She and Brindle help put the mats away and get ready to close up the studio. They eat their sandwiches in the car on the way to the theater.

After buying tickets at the little window out front, they go inside to the counter for their free popcorn. In the darkness, they find seats near the back and settle in just as the movie begins. It's a film with knights and princesses and medieval plot twists, hunters in the forest, a lavish castle on a hillside, beautiful horses, and a handsome hero. Deanne feels like she lives in this other world so much of the time now. Between dancing in *Giselle*, reading *Pride and Prejudice*, and watching historical fiction movies, she's pretty well immersed in this alternate reality. Sometimes it's more real to her than her normal, everyday life. Or at least, she wishes it was.

Brindle groans when the hero falls off his horse and Willow says, "Get back on. Hurry up!"

"Shh." Miss Val puts her hand on her daughter's knee.

Willow's friend giggles and spills half her popcorn on the floor.

Deanne watches Brindle roll her eyes. "Little sisters and their friends," she says, shaking her head.

Deanne puts her head in her hands during the thick of the battle scene. She isn't up to witnessing much blood and gore tonight. She's bloated and still has cramps since starting her period yesterday. How fortunate that it came before the dress rehearsal and performances. At least she won't have to worry about that when showtime arrives.

Deanne thanks Miss Val when she drops her off at home after the movie. "Bye, Brindle. See you at school tomorrow."

What a fun day it's been, but now she yawns and looks forward to going to bed. She isn't even going to read first. Sleep beckons her. Perhaps dreams of faraway places will carry her through the night and let her live in the fantasy world a little bit longer.

But it isn't to be. As soon as Deanne walks inside, Mother meets her at the door.

"How was the movie, Deanne? I hope you enjoyed it. Why don't you put your backpack on the couch? Your father's waiting for you."

What's going on? Deanne dumps her stuff on the sofa and nervously enters the dining room, where Father is sitting at the head of the table. He's fiddling with a small blue box and nods for her to sit down. She's already grounded for sneaking out with her new church friends, so this really confuses her.

Father clears his throat and looks directly into her eyes. "A father's love is very strong and protective, Deanne." He pauses as if for effect. "As is God's."

Another suspended moment of silence stretches out, making her squirm. Deanne hears ticking from the grandfather clock in the living room and the palms of her clamped hands begin to perspire.

"I'm not proud of you for sneaking out like you did with those kids. You do know that was wrong, don't you?"

She nods.

"But at least you told us about it and didn't go through with it. And Deanne, there's something else." He stares sternly at her.

What now?

"You want to *save* yourself and be pure—for God, right?" He stops again and looks down at the box in his hands. "And for your future husband, of course."

She nods tentatively.

He slowly pushes the box toward her. "This is a purity ring. You wear it on your ring finger, to remind you of your promise—to *me* and to *God*—that you'll wait until marriage."

Father's eyes bore into her. She is barely breathing. Her hands tremble as she removes the lid and carefully pulls out a silver band with the engraving, *I'll wait.* She's seen a few girls at church wearing them and feels, in her heart of hearts, that waiting *is* important. She had no idea her own father would give one to her, especially before she's even in high school. *Maybe I scared him a little with my sneaking out episode.* She slides the ring onto her finger and can't help but smile. It fits perfectly.

"Thank you, Father."

"You promise now, right?"

She does. And after repeating the vow of promising to wait, she stands up to hug him.

"Atta girl. Now, off to bed. It's getting late. And Deanne? *Always* remember your promise."

After grabbing her backpack off the couch, she heads upstairs. She is becoming a woman. Not just a little girl anymore, but an adult—with heavy responsibilities.

14

LAST FULL BALLET REHEARSAL

Deanne

*If you forget what comes next,
don't stop. Just make it up.*

It's now June, time for the last of the four full dance rehearsals at the studio in which all the ballet students meet to weave the entire structure of the story together. The Advanced class, as usual, is first so the most experienced dancers can work on their parts before the others arrive.

"Five minutes until *barre*," Miss Val announces. "Randi, you were the first one to arrive. Which exercise do you choose?"

"I'll take *ronde de jambes*."

"How about you, Paige?"

"Hmmm. *Grand battements*."

Sometimes Miss Val allows them to take turns leading their own short *barre* when they're into full rehearsals and warm-ups have to be brief. "Annie? *Pliés* for you, and *tendús* and *dégagés* for Brindle. Deanne? You get *frappés.*"

"Oh goodie," Deanne exaggerates, jumping up and down excitedly. That's her favorite one, with its sharp, staccato beats. She'll show everyone how good she is. *I'll think up the most complicated pattern so even Randi won't get it right.*

The students carry the *barres* out to the center while Todd circles his bum ankle methodically.

"How's it feeling, Todd?" asks Miss Val.

"It's good," he says, hopping around on it. "It hardly hurts at all anymore."

Too bad it's not Randi's ankle. Maybe then I'd get to be Giselle. Deanne knows it isn't very *Christian* to feel this way, but she can't help it.

"Good, that's great. Let's keep it that way, okay? Don't jump around on it so much and make sure to warm it up extra well." She walks over to the sound system and starts the music for *pliés,* after Annie demonstrates her exercise.

When it's time for Deanne to show *frappés,* she flexes her foot and strikes the floor. "Front, side, back, side, then doubles *en croix.* It's a difficult pattern so pay attention." She looks directly at Randi, feeling emboldened, and demonstrates her tricky routine, finishing with, "and balance in *relevé,* leg in *a la seconde,* with arms out."

Randi and the others actually manage to execute Deanne's *frappés* without any problems, but during another exercise involving *glissades* in a box pattern, Deanne gets confused and looks up to copy Randi and notices she's moving differently. *Is she favoring her right foot? If not, then she's doing the same thing that Miss Val sometimes gets on me about. She's not putting her heel down. Why doesn't Miss Val get on HER case about it?*

The group finishes the center stretches on their own and then gets into position to begin Act One. Deanne observes Randi noticeably blushing when Jack takes her hands. *Hmm, interesting.* She wonders if there's something going on there. *A little stage chemistry? Or is it something more?* They run through the various dances before the younger students arrive and work on the variations and duets. During the break, they all sit down for water and snacks to fuel up for the full rehearsal.

The Beginning and Intermediate dance students file in after Miss Val instructs them to leave their shoes outside, since space inside is limited. The tap and hip hop groups have dances that stand alone as entertainment for the festival scene, so they don't need to attend the full rehearsals at the studio.

The students sit on the floor in a large circle, with a few younger ballerinas between each Advanced dancer. Randi begins leading, circling her ankles and flexing and pointing her feet. When it's Deanne's turn, she encourages everyone to sit in a straddle and stretch over each leg.

"Move over!" shouts Lisa, the Intermediate dancer with an attitude.

"Oh, I'm sorry. I can scoot back a little," says a polite, little ballerina, sliding backward to make her part of the circle slightly larger.

Willow reaches forward and touches her forehead to the floor.

"Show off."

"You don't have to have a cow," Willow's tomboy friend says.

Jack tells everyone to stand up quickly and do thirty jumping jacks, which gets everybody smiling. And Annie centers them with *pliés, relevés,* and *port-de-bras.* After warm-ups, Deanne overhears Miss Val talking with Randi.

"What's going on with your heel? I've noticed you've been favoring it lately."

Deanne's nemesis looks nervous. *What's going on?*

Randi picks up her foot and presses on the bottom of it. "It's much better than it was. I hardly feel it at all after warming up."

"Well, what happened?" Miss Val asks, inching closer.

Deanne watches her lean in as Randi whispers into her ear.

Miss Val pulls back. "Oh my gosh! Really? Is it going to be all right?"

"Yeah, the doctor said it is," Randi says with a nervous laugh.

"Well, you need to tell me these kinds of things, Randi! Our whole ballet could be at stake over something like this. Frankly, I'm a little worried. Maybe Deanne should have been stepping in more."

What's that about? Randi and Paige look at each other, and whatever it is, it seems like Paige already knows about it. Deanne suddenly realizes there's now a chance she might actually get to dance the lead! She imagines herself leaping and turning around the dance floor with Jack, and the audience applauding wildly. But then, her fantasy is cut short when Miss Val claps her hands loudly. She looks mad.

"Everyone, in your places to walk through Act One with counts! And then we'll do it with music. Come on, everybody!" Miss Val pauses, as if to compose herself, then asks Annie to pass out the Wili weeds. "Remember to hold the sprigs in your right hands."

Deanne notices Annie give an extra big one to Lisa. *Probably hoping to wipe the scowl off her face.* She *chassés* over to pester Brindle and tickles her neck with a Wili weed. Her friend giggles and moves into place to begin the dance of the Wilis.

All the girls float around Giselle, initiating her into their ghostly world—to the place where these fair maidens have perished of broken hearts and become ethereal beings who dance young, unsuspecting men to their untimely deaths if they happen to trespass by the lake at night. The Beginners sit across the front, spellbound by the fluid motions of these dancers they look up to and aspire to become. The little girls laugh hysterically when Todd keeps falling down and eventually collapses for the last time. Deanne can't help but laugh, too. Later, they look on solemnly as Jack and Randi perform their last duet. The Wilis slowly disappear and Albrecht is left clutching Giselle's cross.

Miss Val calls Randi and Jack to the center to practice their last *pas de deux* together one more time, so Deanne walks forward to dance behind them. When Randi performs her double *pirouette*, with Jack spotting her from behind, Deanne slows her single turn down and ends on a flat foot so she can hold the position at the end—mirroring Randi. During the *penché arabesque*, which Randi executes *en pointe* with Jack's support, Deanne performs this on flat. But she makes sure to extend her leg up higher than Randi's ever goes, hoping Miss Val will take note and be more ready to insert her into the role of prima ballerina.

As the cast practices the finale bows, the costume lady comes in with armloads of white, gauzy garments; colorful peasant dresses; and green hunter tunics, which she puts near the other costumes that hang in the back of the studio. They're all neatly wrapped and organized into categories. It's so exciting; the pieces of their production are coming together.

Miss Val seats the students on the floor in their respective groups and invites the parents to come in and sit on the low balance beam the boys have brought out, stand, or sit on the floor. This is the parent meeting before the show. She gives them handouts with all the pertinent information, but Miss Val holds this meeting to personally touch base with everyone she can. Deanne hears her ask certain people to help with the concert. She explains, "This kind of performance—a story ballet—entails a little more coordination than a regular recital. We need more volunteers backstage, help with refreshments, and chaperones to sit with students in the audience. Lots of jobs. Please let me know if you can help out in any way. It truly does take a village. Also, I'd like to thank you all for loaning me your children. They're really terrific." She continues with information such as who should bring cookies or juice, based on what letter their last name begins with; that it's important for everyone, except the Advanced dancers, to leave their shoes and extra things with the parents in the audience since space is limited backstage; and call times for dress rehearsal, assembly performance, and concert, finishing with, "Thank you all, again, and we'll see you next week!"

A mom's hand goes up. "Miss Val?"

"Yes?"

"I just want you to know how much I really appreciate all you do for our kids. I don't know how you get these little ones to do what they do, but we all really appreciate you." The lady turns around, addressing the other parents. "Don't we?" She looks around at the group.

"We sure do," a dad says and everyone starts clapping.

JP, the assistant, comes forward, also clapping her hands. "Miss Val is very good at what she does. And one of the reasons she has these full rehearsals, besides to practice together, is to get everyone used to each other while performing in front of other people. Plus, it helps to lessen their stage fright before they ever even go up on stage. I don't know if any other studio does this."

Miss Val raises her hands as the parents begin applauding again. "Thanks, you guys. But we're already going overtime and I know you all are busy, so—Mrs. Flanners?"

The costume lady rises from the chair at the desk and helps Miss Val hand out the costume bags with the performers' names on them.

Addressing the younger students and their parents, Miss Val says, "Your costumes are to stay in these bags in your moms' closets until dress rehearsal. These are rental costumes and are not to be played with. Okay?" Miss Val glances at each of the Beginners authoritatively and then smiles.

Deanne watches Lisa frown when Mrs. Flanners hands her a pale green dress. "I wanted a red one."

Miss Val marches over. "We don't always get our first choice color. We have to be good sports. Mrs. Flanners worked very hard on your dress, so why don't you thank her?"

She looks up and says quietly, "Thank you," and sets the costume in her lap.

The dancer sitting next to her leans over and says, "I think yours is beautiful."

"Well, that's easy for you to say. Yours is red."

Willow's friend rises and holds a bright yellow peasant dress against her front, admiring herself in the mirror. Willow laughs, and then they all start to stand up.

"All right. Enough, girls. Let's keep it under wraps or we'll have chaos break loose," Miss Val says, handing out the last costume bag. "Make sure you don't go outside without a parent and I'll see you all at dress rehearsal!"

Deanne waits until the line of parents with questions for Miss Val dissipates and then approaches her. She feels hopeful now that Randi's injured—or something, of maybe getting to step in for her.

"Miss Val?"

"Yes, Deanne?"

"I was wondering. Um. Do you think I should start rehearsing more with Jack now that Randi's heel is bothering her?" She tries to keep her voice steady, feigning concern.

Miss Val glances toward the last Beginner leaving the studio with her father before turning back to Deanne. "It looks like Randi will be all right, but thanks for asking. I think we'll be okay." She sets down a stack of flyers on the desk and clears her throat. "Oh, and Deanne?" She pauses. "I know how excited you are to be the understudy, but you've got to give Randi some breathing room. This is all new for her, too, you know? Dancing the lead and all. Let's show her some support, okay?"

Deanne's heart weighs heavy and her eyes begin to sting—the precursor to tears, but she fights them back.

Miss Val must recognize the need to change the subject because she asks if her father will be coming to see her perform.

It must be obvious to everyone how he's never there. Too busy with more important things.

"If he can," Deanne answers. At least she hopes so. A tear escapes and she wipes her cheek.

Deanne gathers her things from underneath the ballet *barres* and walks out front with the other Advanced dancers. Jack takes off on his bicycle and Todd hitches a ride from Annie. Sophia's mother shoos her gazillion children into the van as Randi and Paige come out of the studio.

"How did the doctor take it out of your foot?" Paige asks.

"With these weird tweezers, I think. I was too scared to watch."

Deanne moves closer. "What happened to your foot, anyway?" She tries to sound more concerned than she really is.

Randi glances at Paige before answering. "I was sewing on my *pointe* shoe ribbons, lost track of the needle, and jumped down off my bed. The whole thing went into my heel."

Deanne fights the urge to barf. "Oh my gosh!" She stands there staring at Randi with her mouth hanging open. "Did it hurt?"

"Huh? Of course it hurt." She takes a moment, then says, "But it didn't really hurt as much as I thought it would've. I guess it didn't hit any nerves."

"Wow. Sorry about that. You must have been worried about not being able to dance, huh?"

Randi frowns. "Yes, I was."

Deanne's head starts to pound. She feels out of breath. Her body begins to convulse and then, she's crying. Huge, unstoppable sobs. Tears stream down her cheeks and thoughts of her father's disappointed tone, when she told him she was not the one dancing the lead, bombard her. And—and—and—when she gets anything lower than an A on her report card. *Will I ever measure up?* And then it hits her that, all season, she's been kind of mean to Randi, and everyone really. And nothing's working out for her. It's all backfiring. The flood of emotions, of everything, suddenly overwhelms her.

Paige touches her shoulder. "Deanne, what's wrong?"

She can't remember ever feeling this discombobulated and out of control. Their faces blur in her field of vision. "I—I—I just. I don't know. I'm so sorry, Randi." She wipes her eyes with the back of her sleeve as her thoughts slowly begin to clarify.

"What are you talking about, Deanne?" Randi's face gets closer.

Deanne wails, "I'm sorry for how I've been to you. You don't deserve it!"

Randi looks confused, but then says, "I do feel like you've been trying, a little too hard sometimes, to replace me."

"I was." More sobs take over. "I just thought that if I got the lead role then my father might actually have something to be proud of me about. I'm such a failure." By now her voice is barely audible.

"That's ridiculous, Deanne," Paige says, moving in to give her a hug. "We're all proud of you here. We're your dance family."

Everyone has congregated now; Paige, Randi, Brindle, and Sophia have enveloped her in a group hug.

"Yeah, silly. We're all proud of you and think you're a wonderful dancer," Brindle says, into her ear.

"But cut us a little slack, huh, Deanne?"

She looks up and sees it's Randi who's spoken.

"Trust us a little, okay? We're not out to get you. It's not a competition."

They all turn to look at Randi.

"Well, not entirely, anyway." She laughs. "Let's just lighten up and enjoy each other, okay?"

"We all love you, Deanne," Paige says.

Deanne can hardly believe this. They're all so nice. And all along she's been putting everyone else down so she can look better. *That really worked out well. Not. It's just made me look weak.*

Luckily, by the time Deanne's mom arrives, she's pulled herself back together, for the most part, anyway.

"See you later, Deanne!" Randi shouts from the group, and waves.

Deanne waves back and gets into the car. She knows the other girls aren't out to get her. It's just that everything has always been a competition to her. She can thank her father for that. But even so, there might still be a chance she could be Giselle. Old habits die hard; so, of course, she'll keep practicing Randi's parts and if the opportunity arises—she'll be ready for it.

"Mother? Can we stop somewhere for dinner on the way home?"

As they pull out of the parking lot, Mother finally answers. "No, not tonight, honey. I've got a stew going in the Crock-Pot at home. Besides, your father's probably already home."

Deanne takes a big gulp from her water bottle, picturing her father lording over their little household. *What a pompous tyrant.* She immediately feels guilty for the thought and leans back in her seat, closing her eyes. During the remainder of the ride home, she ponders the big-heartedness of her dance family and what a needle in her foot might feel like. Not pleasant, she's sure.

15

FAMILY OBLIGATIONS

Randi

Pretend that you already can!

Randi is not looking forward to missing this Saturday's ballet class, but she has no choice in the matter. But perhaps the rest will allow her almost-healed foot to recover the rest of the way. It hasn't been nearly as big a deal as she'd feared, but it still isn't one hundred percent and she has to make sure she's super warmed up before it stops hurting. Maybe it's the natural pain-killing effect of those endorphins released during exercise. Her second (or is it third?) cousin is getting married this weekend, in Phoenix, and her parents insisted they all attend even though they really don't know her that well. Today is Thursday, and after school they'll finish packing and leave early tomorrow morning. Not that she loves school, but she hates to miss classes this close to finals.

It makes things more difficult. Packing her books is a no brainer.

During lunch Paige asks, "Are you going to get to do some of the driving? It's a long way to Arizona; you could get a lot of practice."

Randi takes a carrot out of her bag and sits for a moment. "Yeah, I think so. My mom said I'd be able to drive in California, I guess, but my permit isn't valid in Arizona."

"Huh. I didn't know that," Paige says. "If I ever get my permit, hopefully this summer, I know I'll need all the practice I can get."

When school lets out, Randi meets David in the parking lot, where he's standing around joking with his friends.

"I told you guys I couldn't be there for tomorrow's game. We've got this wedding to go to in Phoenix."

"Sure, man. See you next week," says the one with the scruffy beard before they wander away.

Randi buckles her seatbelt and David squeals out of the lot. "Hey, slow down! I'll tell Mom."

"Oh, shut up. You're such a wimp. I can't believe you're not dying to get *your* license. I got mine as soon as I could. Wheels are my freedom!"

"Well, I'm not you, David." She wishes she could feel as confident as her brother seems to be.

He rolls down the window and yells, "Hey!" to a group of girls walking home, and they wave back flirtatiously. He drives to a house near the park and drops off Randi to babysit.

She rings the doorbell and the mom answers the door, holding her toddler.

"Oh good, you're here. I shouldn't be long, only a couple of hours. He's already eaten and probably just wants to play." The woman kisses the little boy and heads out to her car.

Randi seizes the moment to distract the child from being upset by his mom leaving. She shakes a little blue rattle around his face and behind his head before letting him have it. When he starts to whimper, "I want Mommy," their little black kitten appears and runs around Randi's legs. The kid forgets all about whining and starts laughing.

Oh no. Not again. The little boy starts chasing the cat around Randi, all the while shrieking, laughing, and pulling the poor thing's tail.

Why doesn't it just go run off and hide somewhere? She feels terrible for the kitty and does her best to protect it, but the child is persistent. It's like this almost every time she babysits for this family. She's surprised the cat is still alive with the kind of torture it gets from this kid.

Finally, she can't stand it anymore and straps him in the stroller and heads to the park for the next hour and a half or so, to pass the time. By then, David should be back to pick her up.

When they get home, Mom is already there, arranging food and accessories for the trip. "Hey, guys. Make sure you get whatever laundry you need done right away so Dad can do his as soon as he gets home tonight." She continues to pull plastic containers out of the cupboard and fills them with nuts, granola, and dried fruit.

Randi thinks she looks tired. She probably is. Her mom has already put in a day aiding kids at school. What a job. She doesn't think that would work for her as a career. Extreme patience is not one of her strong suits. At least, not enough for that job.

The following morning at 5:00 a.m., Randi's alarm clock rings and she presses the snooze button. She loses track of how many times, but finally gives in to the building pressure. Luckily, she beats David to the bathroom and jumps in the shower.

"Hurry up!" her brother yells, knocking loudly on the hollow core door.

"Don't get your panties in a bundle!" she teases. Randi takes her time dressing and then methodically brushes her teeth. Why not give him back some of his own annoying medicine. He never hurries for her.

Mom calls for them to "Get a move on!"

Randi comes out of the bathroom and gives David a snide smirk.

"I hope you're going to drive us in a more grown-up manner than how you're acting right now," he says, pushing past her and closing the door behind him.

"Ha!" She's going to get to drive at least part of the way today, but can't help being nervous.

The family finishes packing the car and is on the road by 7:15 a.m., only fifteen minutes behind schedule. It rained all night and hasn't stopped all morning, and the road has become a shallow river. Randi leans over the steering wheel, peering through sheets of water interrupted by the rapid motion of the windshield wipers. Her knuckles whiten, and her hands cramp.

"Dad, please let me drive," David says. "She's gonna kill us all."

"The weather is a bit much, honey. A little rain is one thing for practicing, but this? Why don't you drive?" Mom finally asks Dad.

After having been coached by all three of her passengers and encouraged to let Dad drive, Randi mutters, "I'm done," slowly exits the freeway, and pulls into a gas station.

"Bathroom breaks, everyone," Dad says. "We'd like to not have to stop again until we're there."

Later that afternoon, they check into a motel and settle into their suite. There's a rollaway bed for David, and Randi gets the sofa bed. Her brother immediately begins flipping channels.

Randi yells, "Turn it down!"

"We have a little over an hour before our dinner reservation. I'm taking a shower now," Mom says, taking a zippered pouch and an armload of clothes with her.

Randi opens her luggage and pulls out the outfit she's going to wear to the wedding. She hangs the pretty red and blue dress in the closet, next to the burgundy one already there. She likes the dresses she and her mom picked out and hopes to get a picture of the two of them together. Dad talks on the phone with someone from work about the place they're going to eat. She surmises that the person is the one who'd recommended it.

"I'll definitely try the lobster," he says before hanging up. He looks at both kids. "The shrimp and oysters are supposed to be really good, too."

"Almost anything sounds good to me," David says. "I'm starving."

"You're always hungry," Randi says.

The restaurant is dimly lit except for the bar near the front. Their dinner is really tasty. They all say so. After finishing the meal, they step outside into the furnace that Phoenix becomes this time of year and hurry back to the air-conditioned motel.

Randi changes into her pajamas and wonders what kind of wedding they're attending tomorrow. She doesn't really know these relatives. Super religious? Pagan? Are they saying their own vows? They haven't talked much about it, other than they were going to go and it's to be held outside. She hopes it won't be unbearably hot.

Before turning off the lamp next to the sofa, Randi decides to call Nana. David is occupied on his iPad, wearing headphones, and her parents are already in the bedroom.

Randi reminds her they're in Arizona and she wishes she could've been there, too. "Oh, and guess what!"

"No telling with you, Coyote. What's up?"

"Well, remember when I told you about that girl trying to steal my role?" Randi thinks for a second before continuing. "It turns out she mostly wanted it so she could impress her overbearing father. She's not quite as conceited as I thought. But I'm still worried. She *is* the understudy, after all."

"What did I tell you? Things are never completely what they seem, are they? And everybody's got a good side no matter how difficult they might be. Right?"

"I guess so, Nana." She loves these conversations. She's so lucky to have someone like her to talk with. "You know, I wonder if Deanne has someone like you to talk to."

"Well Randi, that person could be you—if she needs it."

"Yeah, I guess maybe it could be." She ponders the idea. "I'll just have to keep an eye out to see what she needs, I guess."

"That's my girl. Well, dear, I'll see you at your big performance. Break a leg and all that good stuff," Nana says, laughing.

David takes off his headphones and glares at her, ending their conversation, and yells, "Goodnight, Nana!"

Luckily, the weather has cooled down a little and Randi's family spends the morning wandering around the ASU campus. David will be graduating soon and then attend SDSU in San Diego in the fall. Randi figures her parents want both of them to get slightly familiar with college campuses before actually leaving home. At least they aren't just sitting around in the motel doing nothing. She appreciates feeling her muscles move and pauses every so often to stretch, putting a leg up onto a planter box or a fence rail, and leaning over it. She only feels her heel once in a while now, mostly when she's barefoot.

By the time they're seated on the white, foldout chairs under a lush garden canopy, Randi is grateful to finally relax. Flowers bloom all around them, and a string quartet plays as guests are seated. It all looks so beautiful. If Randi ever gets married, she'll want it to be just like this. Thoughts of Jack drift through her head. *He is awfully cute. And nice, too. Does he ever think of me that way?* And then, everyone stands when the bride and her father walk down the aisle. She looks stunning. Her simply cut gown drapes gracefully over her body, showing off her attractive figure.

Following a reading from *The Prophet*, the musicians begin to play again. Dancers in flowing dresses waltz in and perform a beautiful contemporary piece. They're really good. The seven women range in age,

Randi figures, from eighteen to forty or so. About a minute into the dance, one of them walks effortlessly up a staircase consisting of the other dancers' laced-together hands or uniquely presented backs. Upon reaching the top, she flies off, getting caught gracefully mid-flight by the original stair step dancers, who have shifted to the other end of the line. It's a pretty tricky move. She'll have to remember that one for the future. They probably worked on it for a long time to be able to pull it off so well.

After the ceremony is over, the wedding party poses in a variety of locations for photographs while the guests mingle and sample hors d'oeuvres and make polite conversation. She and David stand around awkwardly, eating fancy crackers with brie. Their Aunt Louise comes over and comments on how grown up they both look, but when a tray of sparkling champagne flutes goes by, she leaves abruptly to follow it.

"I always heard she was a lush," David says, raising his eyebrows as they watch her grab not one, but two glasses from the server.

A group of girls comes over to introduce themselves to David, giggling nervously. Of course, her brother flirts disgustingly with all of them. Randi feels herself being edged out and walks over to look at the fountain. She recognizes one of the dancers standing on the other side.

"I loved your dance."

"Thank you," she laughs. "The bride asked us to perform only a month ago."

"Wow. You guys were able to pull that off in a month? I'm impressed. By the way, I'm Randi."

"I'm Laurie. Do you dance?"

"Yes. I take ballet at a studio in the San Diego area. That's where I live."

Laurie adjusts her handbag over her shoulder. "Wow. Ballet, huh? That's hard stuff. How long have you been dancing?"

Randi feels the edge of the fountain for dampness and then sits down gingerly. She follows Laurie's series of questions and answers accordingly. She also tells her about dancing the part of Giselle. She doesn't know why, but she feels very relaxed around this young woman.

"You must be pretty good to get the lead role."

Randi shifts to face her. "Oh, I don't know about that. The girl who should have gotten the lead—" She thinks for a moment before continuing. "She left, so I guess I was next in line."

Notes from a violin serve as background to their conversation and influences Randi's response when Laurie suggests how fun it must be to get to do *pas de deux* at her age.

If she only knew. "Well," she begins. "To tell you the truth, I'm having a really hard time with it."

The way this woman listens—it's almost like a big sister might.

"For one thing," Randi begins. "There's an understudy for my part and she's really good. I feel like if I don't pull it together soon, she's going to get to be Giselle."

"Well, there's always someone waiting in the wings, isn't there?" Laurie trails her fingers through the water behind them. "That never goes away no matter what you're doing: jobs, school, you know—whatever."

"Yeah, I guess so. But on top of that," Randi pauses before sharing how insecure and flustered she gets when Jack touches her for partnering, and how difficult it is to learn such intricate steps at the same time. They speak in hushed tones while the solo instrument continues to play.

"You know what, Randi? I'm twenty-eight and I can tell you right now that those feelings never totally go away. You just get more used to them." Laurie rummages through her purse and pulls out her cell phone. "You gotta see this." She flips through images on the screen. "Here it is."

Randi leans over and there Laurie is, in a horizontal stag, held up in the air by one guy. When she taps the screen, Randi watches her being dropped, rolling through the air, and then caught in a pose similar to a fish dive.

Randi gasps. "How on earth did you learn that? Weren't you scared? It looks absolutely terrifying."

"Yeah, sure I was scared. But we practiced it a lot and then were able to nail it most of the time. It's not as big a deal as it looks."

Randi straightens up and glances around. *Is this woman for real? Yes. Of course she is. She's sitting right here beside me.* The water trickles gently behind them, spit out by a green cement fish. "I don't think I could ever do that."

"Oh, don't kid yourself. It's just a state of mind. And a lot of work." Laurie laughs. "And once you make a decision to do something, it can be that simple. You just decide to do it." She glances at her phone. "I have to go. I think you'll do perfectly fine as Giselle." The lady stands up and begins to walk away, but turns back to wave. "Hey, remember. State of mind." She points her finger to her forehead and leaves smiling.

Just do it? It's not that simple.

Randi hears the DJ announcing the new couple and encouraging everyone to find their assigned seats. Randi's family joins other relatives, most of whom she's only met a few times before. Candles and small mason jars overflowing with colorful flowers decorate the tables, which are set at various angles to each other. The first course, salad, is followed by either a chicken or vegetarian lasagna, depending on what had been pre-ordered when RSVPing.

"Randi is dancing the lead in *Giselle*. She's become such a beautiful dancer."

Randi looks up with a mouthful of chicken when she hears her mother's voice.

"You must be so proud," Aunt Louise says, pausing to take a large gulp of red wine. "And you, my dear, to be Giselle. You must be so excited."

Randi quickly swallows and nods. "Mm hmm."

David rolls his eyes and groans.

The best man stands up at the wedding party's table and taps a spoon against his champagne glass. "I'd like to toast the bride and groom. Long may they be united!"

The usual cake cutting, bouquet throwing, garter tossing, and dancing proceed seamlessly. Randi appreciates the choreography, and most likely the rehearsals and obvious attention to details that this production must have gone through. It is a performance, of sorts. Not unlike a stage production. She's impressed.

That night, after everyone else has gone to bed, she talks to Paige on her cell phone and tells her about the contemporary dance in the ceremony and how beautiful everything was.

"And you should have seen David. He thinks he's so cool. He flirted and fawned over this group of girls that came up to him." It's great to be able to talk with her best friend, who really knows her. After filling her in on the details of the wedding, she closes with, "I'll see you Monday."

She turns off her phone and puts her head down on the pillow, thinking through the dance steps in her solo. She pictures Miss Val reminding them to do this before they go to sleep so the subconscious can be a partner in remembering the dance. Randi wonders if this is part of that state of mind thing the young woman had talked to her about earlier today.

16

DRESS REHEARSAL

Deanne

*Visualize going through the
movements before going to sleep.*

Deanne walks into the Performing Arts Center, loaded down with her dance bag, costumes, makeup kit, extra clothes, and accessories. Mother serves as her Sherpa, carrying snacks and water. Brindle hurries down the stage steps to meet them and Sophia trudges in, her tiny form almost buried under her own pile of belongings.

"You can put your things in the dressing room and start helping out," Miss Val calls from up on the scaffolding, tying the last knot to secure the valance over the village backdrop. "The stage needs a good sweeping."

"I can do that," Deanne's mother says. "Where would you like these snacks?"

"Let's put those in the auditorium. I don't want the younger kids eating back here." Miss Val climbs down, and she and Mr. Val push the scaffolding to the center of the stage so the technician can adjust a light. "Jethro, could you help him for a while?" Mr. Val always pitches in during the performance season.

Taz tags along. He enthusiastically helps push the scaffolding and carries stage lights.

"Come on, son. Let's do this." Mr. Val smiles at him.

There's always so much to be done to get the stage ready. Deanne hears Miss Val say that she and her husband had hung the backdrop earlier that day with the stage manager, who was a Dance Centre student several years ago and comes each year to help out. Two mom volunteers are safety-pinning the rips in the huge black curtain that closes across the back of the stage. The custodian orders everyone off the floor for half an hour so he can mop. The crew moves down to the seating area and begins setting up more chairs in the expansive room.

By and by, more students and parents arrive and Miss Val reminds them to keep their things in the audience area, since only the Advanced dancers, or those with multiple roles, will have access to the dressing rooms. She is emphatic that everyone keeps their stuff contained and not leave it haphazardly around the stage.

"What's that ring on your finger? Is it new?" Brindle asks Deanne.

"Yes, it's a promise ring my father gave me."

Brindle squints at it. "Huh?"

Deanne interrupts her. "Oh, I almost forgot. I got you guys presents!" She doesn't feel like explaining the ring to Brindle right now anyway. She probably wouldn't understand.

"What? Why?" Brindle asks, following Deanne and Sophia into the dressing room.

Sophia jiggles excitedly when Deanne reaches into her bag and pulls out two small pink packages. She watches them each lift out a sparking ballerina necklace; they both squeal with delight.

"Oh you shouldn't have," Sophia says and gives her a hug.

"Thank you so much. You're so thoughtful." Brindle smiles and carefully lowers the gift back into its wrapping and slips it into her dance bag.

"You're welcome," Deanne says, smiling at her two best friends. "Let's get back out there, you guys. I'm so excited it's finally dress rehearsal."

Miss Val is going over stage notes with the stage manager, the technician who runs sound and lights with Mr. Val's assistance, and the parent volunteers who'll be helping backstage. They huddle together, taking notes on the outlines Miss Val has provided. Deanne marvels at how organized it all is.

An hour and a half later, JP takes charge of painting brown circles on the preschool gymnasts' noses to make them look like forest animals. They're so cute in their costumes, scurrying around getting into mischief. Deanne startles when JP claps her hands and directs the gymnasts to find their assigned places, in the left section of the audience, where they'll sit while not actually on stage performing.

In the dressing room, the Advanced girls frantically apply makeup, adjust costumes, and banter excitedly.

"Ooh, can I use that eyeliner? Mine's almost gone." Paige rifles through her bag, then dumps the contents onto the counter. "I must not have any more."

"Sure," Deanne says. She loans her the tube even though she'd rather not share. "Just give it back when you're done, okay?"

Two Beginning girls come in with their mom, wearing cute little peasant dresses.

"Hello. They're not supposed to be in here," Randi says. "Miss Val said only the Advanced dancers and the girls with multiple roles."

"Oh, I didn't realize," the mom says. "Come on, girls. We have to go out." She has to coax them away. They're mesmerized by the older girls' dress-up activity.

Randi apologizes to the mom for kicking them out. "It's just what Miss Val told us to do," and she turns back to the mirror and brushes black mascara onto her already thick lashes.

"Oh, my goodness!" Paige shrieks. "Look what I did." The eyeliner is running down the inside corners of her eyes and onto her cheeks.

"Oops. I forgot to tell you that it's extra thin and runny."

"That would've helped." Paige giggles good-naturedly and wipes the black rivers from her face.

"I'm so nervous," Sophia pants, brushing rouge over her cheekbones. "Aren't you?"

"Don't get me started," Randi snaps. "Keep it to yourself." Then she smiles. "Please?"

At last it's time to begin the dress rehearsal. The whole cast, except the littlest gymnasts, begin backstage since they're all in Act One. Even the tap dancers and hip-hoppers are there, since they provide the gypsy entertainment for the village celebration.

The scene opens onto the festivities of the grape harvest, with the entire village dancing, including Giselle. Her mother, Berthe, worries when her weak-hearted daughter dances with a man known as Loys. He is, of course, Prince Albrecht in disguise.

Deanne watches Annie feign concern for Randi as Jack twirls her around quickly. The little tap dancers clomp across the stage humorously, entertaining the guests with their chaotic cadences. Even Miss Val chuckles when she has to start the music over again for them to repeat their dance. After a few more snags, Act One ends and the cast prepares for Act Two.

Deanne and the other Advanced dancers drink water and change costumes as the crew swaps the backdrops. Act Two will be the night scene at the lake. Deanne walks through the Wili steps with Brindle and Sophia; she notices Jack sitting down on stage left leaning against the wall. He doesn't look well. When Randi comes over and offers him some water, he perks up and smiles.

"I think she likes him," Deanne blurts out before realizing it. *And everybody likes Randi. Why can't I be more like her?*

Sophia turns and looks. "I think the feeling's mutual."

"Come on, you guys. Let's finish our walkthrough before Act Two starts," Brindle says, executing the *balancé entournants* moving toward stage right.

Deanne says, "Go ahead; I'll catch up with you. She walks behind the back curtain and begins marking through Randi's Act Two dances—just in case.

"Places, everyone!" Miss Val calls. "Jack, do you feel well enough to continue?"

"Yeah, I'm okay. I need the practice," he says, and slowly gets up and ambles over to stage left.

The music begins and the curtains open. The Wilis initiate Giselle into the sisterhood, led by Annie, who's the Queen Willi, Myrthe. As Willow's friend loops her arm through Lisa's, their sleeves catch and snag apart, leaving both garments dragging a thin, gauze tail.

"Keep going!" Miss Val shouts over the music. "Remember the rule. Don't stop for anything. Just pretend it didn't happen."

Both girls scowl at each other and Deanne rolls her eyes and glares at them.

"It could have happened to you, you know," Randi says as Willow loops through.

Just then, Annie accidentally kicks a water bottle across the floor, spilling the contents along its path. "I'm sorry, Miss Val. I didn't mean to."

The Beginners in the audience explode into laughter and Miss Val walks out onto the apron, the very front part of the stage, waving her arms up at the booth for them to stop the music. One of the stage moms quickly mops the floor with paper towels while the Act Two dancers sit down for a mild scolding. Miss Val keeps a positive spin on it, though. The costume lady comes backstage and pins the Wili's sleeves back together and Deanne wonders if anything more will go wrong tonight. *If only Randi's foot, or toe—anything, will twist or sprain or something, so I can dance the lead role. I'll keep watch and dance as well as I can.*

"First of all, I need everyone to focus and do your very best. As funny as ripping costumes may be, you've got to keep it to yourselves. We want this to look like a real nighttime scene where you Wilis are roping Giselle in as one of your own. No more goofing around! Got it? We don't want to be here all night." She signals them all back to their beginning places and Act Two starts again.

Things proceed fairly smoothly for a while until Jack accidently drops Randi at the bottom of the fish dive. No one is hurt since they're both so close to the ground when it happens. Jack just petered out and crumpled to the ground with her.

Maybe this is my chance. I move forward to make myself available. "Would you like me to step in, Miss Val?"

Miss Val enters from the left wing, shaking her head. "No. Let's give them another chance, Deanne."

They resume where they left off when the music restarts. Miss Val is not going to have them repeat it since everyone's tired and Jack is feverish. They run through the finale twice because this is the first time the entire cast rehearses it all together.

After the last bow, Miss Val reminds them to be back in the morning for the assembly when they'll perform for an elementary school coming for a field trip. "This is a performance, but it's also an extra practice for our concert tomorrow night." She looks at all the littlest dancers. "It'll be so much fun!" She rubs her hands together excitedly. "And Jack? Go home and get to bed! We *need* you tomorrow."

Most of the students and parents are now leaving, carrying costumes and dragging sleepy children out of the theater. The stage crew organizes props and changes backdrops for tomorrow's assembly. Deanne and her mother walk out as Miss Val's family comes back in for the last load. Deanne is worn out, but excited. She can hardly believe that the concert is tomorrow!

17

SCHOOL ASSEMBLY

Randi

Dance like your life depends on it!

Randi fidgets with the netting under her dress. Even though she's wearing tights, it's still scratchy at the seam between the bodice and skirt. She remembers she packed a nude, spaghetti-strapped leotard and quickly changes, wearing it underneath her dress. *Much better.*

"What a great idea," Willow's tomboy friend says. "I'll have to remember that for tonight. I think I have a tank leotard at home."

"Me too," Willow says, lifting her skirt up and itching her middle. They're in the girls' dressing room backstage.

"Why do you have your Wili costume on? We're peasants first." The girl stares at her friend.

"Oops," Willow says, suddenly startled, but then laughs and changes into the correct outfit.

The performers mill around backstage until Miss Val announces warm-ups and JP takes over. Randi and the other Advanced ballet students are allowed to warm themselves up in a group off to the side or on their own. Their preparations for dancing are different than the others. Doing *pointe* work requires intricate exercises for the feet and legs: *pliés, relevés, tendus, dégagés, ronde de jambes, frappés, fondus,* and *grand battements.*

Annie leans over to her right and then her left, forcing the arch on each foot. "It feels really weird without Bree here, doesn't it?"

Randi comes up from a *grand plié.* "It does. We always had her to lean on. It didn't feel like I had to dance quite as well with her around. If I forgot what step came next I could just, like, watch her."

"It must be kind of scary, huh? I mean, having to lead all this and dance on your own?" Sophia asks.

Deanne jumps up and down doing *changements.* "I think you're lucky to dance the lead. I hope I get to soon."

"I'm sure you'll get your chance," Randi says impatiently. "I just miss Bree. Right now, she'd be coming over and calming us all down and telling us not to worry. Remember how she used to say when we got nervous to just imagine everyone in the audience being naked?"

Todd laughs. "She used to say that at school, too, at our dance production concerts." He pats the back of his head, a common occurrence, to make sure his dreadlocks are in place.

Annie nods. "I hope we'll see her again." She bends over to retie her *pointe* shoe. "Do you feel better today, Jack?"

He crosses his legs and leans down. "Yup, I'm good." He comes up smiling.

"Are you sure?" Randi asks. He still looks a little pale.

"Places, everyone!" Miss Val calls. "Remember, we're performing for an elementary school this morning. They'll love it. So have fun with this, okay?" She smiles and helps the volunteer parents get their groups of children in the right places for the show to begin. When everyone is where they need to be, she takes the microphone and walks out front, parting the front curtains to squeeze through.

Randi listens to their teacher welcome the children to their production of *Giselle*. She says that this presentation is *literature in action* and begins telling them the story of how Giselle loves a prince who is already engaged to someone else. "But she doesn't know that. There is another man, Hilarion, who finds out and tries to warn her, since he loves her, too, but she doesn't believe him." Miss Val goes on to describe the Wilis dancing the men to death, or exhaustion, and how there will be forest animals and hunters. "All those things that appear in so many fairy tales." Randi hears the audience laugh every so often and she can tell the auditorium must be packed.

Miss Val comes back through the voluminous red curtains and whispers, "Are you all ready?" They nod, so she tells the stage manager, who stands next to her wearing a headset, to inform the tech people in the booth to start the music.

Pretty soon, notes drift from the stage monitors and the cast comes to life. The curtains open onto the beautiful scene, resplendent with green vines draped over rustic poles above, and Giselle dances around merrily with the whole village, celebrating the grape harvest. The youngest villagers carry clusters of purple, plastic grapes, and serpentine in a line, in and out of the older groups. Randi looks up at the backdrop of the antiquated village, brightly lit from the stage lights, as she slowly waltzes around another fair maiden and feels like she truly is in that place, as Giselle, over a century ago. Jack smiles at her warmly and their *pas de deux* begins. He swoops her up for a glorious lift and sets her down gently into a split. The gypsies bop on from stage left as entertainment at the celebration.

While the festivities supposedly continue offstage, a large group of hunters enter and meet up with Albrecht. Randi watches from the wings as the gymnasts fly through the air and stalk imaginary prey. The villagers come back on and Giselle becomes fast friends with Bathilda, Albrecht's fiancée. When Giselle learns the truth, she dies in her lover's arms of a broken heart. Hilarion and Albrecht turn on each other in rage before the prince flees the scene in misery. The curtains close as Berthe, Giselle's mother, weeps over her daughter's body.

Miss Val informs everyone to quickly and quietly get ready for Act Two, and Randi watches her go back out between the front curtains to talk to the children in the audience. The forest animals come backstage while the Advanced students, and the others who need to change costumes, file into the dressing room.

"Did you see me slip? I almost fell down!" Deanne pants.

Such drama.

"No, when?" Brindle asks, slipping her peasant dress onto a wire hanger.

"I saw it. I almost ran over you," Sophia says, breezing past and removing her head wreath.

"Shh. We have to be quiet," Annie warns, unzipping the back of her dress.

Paige puts on her Wili gown and helps Randi pull her dress over her head without messing up her hair. "This is so much fun." She laughs. "I was so nervous earlier, but now I'm having a blast!"

Randi giggles along with her.

"Shh," Annie says again, smiling. "You guys are too much."

The stage manager pokes her head in the door. "You girls almost ready?"

"Almost," Randi answers. "I just have to redo my lipstick."

"Okay. In five," she says and gently closes the door.

When Act Two begins, Randi soars through the air—*sauté, tombé, glissade, grand pas de chat*—dancing her prince toward his demise. She and her sister Wilis have already done in Hilarion. Now it's Albrecht's turn. But her character, Giselle, can't do it. She loves him too much.

Waiting in the wings, Randi frantically shakes her head, arms, and legs, attempting to get rid of her tension. *Why am I so nervous? Well, at least it's not the evening concert. Let it go.* The Fresnel lantern on stage left shines with hot, red light, heating her back, and her tight muscles begin to let go. *Ah, this feels good. Wish I could stay here.* Her heel feels almost back to normal. She mouths, "Five, six, seven, eight," and runs out to center stage. Swooping around Jack, she notices him sweating profusely. *Is he still sick?*

She finishes her last *balancé en tournant* and arrives at his side. When he offers his gleaming hand, she reluctantly takes it for support in her slow attitude turn. Her fingers gradually slide from his grip, forcing her to end the tour prematurely in *soussus. He needs to wipe his hands. How do I tell him?*

They circle around, following the line of Wilis and stop to prepare for their diagonal crossing. Standing in B-plus, Randi takes a deep breath and blows upward to dislodge the stray hair on her forehead, unsuccessfully. Jack places his hands slightly above her hips and she feels them shake. *Uh oh.* When the music crescendo begins, they travel across the floor with him lifting her higher with each passing step: *sauté, tombé, glissade, saut de chat.* It feels pretty strong. *Okay. This is working now.* Even the fish dive goes well.

Randi and the other Wilis continue to dance the prince toward his demise, increasing the tempo of their circling and leaping. As the nerve-wracking shoulder sit approaches, Randi notices again how much Jack is sweating. *I better do as much of the work myself as possible or I won't make it all the way up to his shoulder.* Forcing negative thoughts from her mind, she positions herself in front of him and prepares for her big jump. *Soussus,* deep *plié.* They whisper, "One, two, THREE," then the huge jump!

Randi pushes off the floor with all her might, gripping his wrists and pressing downward. She can barely hold on they're so slippery with sweat. She squeezes tighter, sailing upward higher than she's ever gone before. *This can't be right.* The back of her knees cling to the front of his right shoulder. *Wait, shouldn't my bottom be on his shoulder?* She feels herself tipping backward, careening toward the backdrop. Everything moves in slow motion. His hand is now behind her, pushing her torso forward. As they go down, he somehow ends up underneath her, cushioning her fall.

Bright lights from above blind her as the circle of young Wilis around them gasp. *Why are the lights in front of me?* She lies on her back, straddled over him. *Am I waking up? Was I taking a nap? No, it's too bright in here. Am I outside?* Then instantly, she knows where she is. On top of Jack! In a completely undignified position! *How embarrassing.* A sharp whistle stops the commotion abruptly. *I must be beet red. Does anyone notice?* Miss Val appears and Randi rolls to her side, uncomfortably, extricating Jack from beneath her. *Is that the narrator speaking? Is he supposed to talk right now?*

"Are you guys alright?" Miss Val asks. Teacher concern registers on her face.

What's Miss Val doing on stage?

Jack turns over onto his stomach before getting to his feet. "I'm fine. Are you okay, Randi?"

Randi stands up slowly and sees that the front curtain is closed. She feels confused and uneasy.

"I think so. But I fell on top of you." She watches the other dancers drift to new positions as Miss Val's voice echoes in her head. Then the sounds turn into words again and Deanne appears in Randi's peripheral vision.

"Do you need me to dance for her?"

Miss Val raises her eyebrows at Randi.

Oh my gosh! I can't let this happen. She shakes her head.

"Deanne," Miss Val says. "No. Not right now. Go back to your place, please." She then instructs Randi and Jack to strike a pose together, instead of performing the dreaded feat again.

When the curtains open, the audience applauds. *Probably showing their appreciation that we're all right.* The cast resumes the ballet where they'd left off, except from the new pose. Randi teeters, weak-kneed and wobbly. Her confidence has been completely destroyed. She dances in a haze, barely aware of what she's doing.

The first rays of dawn cast light across the lake and the Wilis vanish. The prince is left, weeping at Giselle's grave. The curtains close, and the audience applauds. All Randi can think about is that frightening fall. How will she be able to do it again tonight at the concert? *Absolutely not! Never again!*

The cast assembles for the finale and enters when the music cues them. Each group comes out and bows before backing up to make room for the next. Randi is the last to come out and curtsy. Then Jack walks forward and sheepishly takes her hand. The entire cast, following their lead, does a final bow in unison.

Miss Val comes onstage and claps for them, too, and thanks the schoolchildren for being such a good audience. "Sometimes accidents happen. Everybody's okay and now the dancers can learn how to do it better for next time."

The curtains close and the cast cheers.

"Good job, everybody! Even you guys," Miss Val says, looking at Randi and Jack. "You completely caught her fall, Jack. That was amazing. I can't believe you were able to do that. Well done. Can you both come early this evening so we can work on that lift?"

They both agree to.

"See you all tonight for the concert!" she announces. "And Jack? Is there any way you could take a nap today and get better before tonight?"

Paige leads Randi into the dressing room. After changing out of her Wili outfit and into her school clothes, Randi hangs up her costumes and organizes her things for that evening.

"I don't think I can ever do that shoulder sit again," Randi says, finally speaking. She and Paige are the last ones left in the dressing room. "That was so scary."

"It looked like it. But he totally took that fall for you," Paige explains.

Why is Paige always able to see the big picture? Sometimes it's annoying. Especially when you just want an ally.

"I know, but it was still awful and embarrassing."

Walking out of the dressing room, they find Miss Val picking up empty water bottles from the side wings.

"Can Randi and I come back here right after school? My mom said she'd bring us dinner and there's not really much time to go home between. Will you be here then?"

"Yes, I'll still be here. We have to reset the stage and backdrop. Plus, I don't want the school lunch crowd coming in here and messing with our stuff." The Performing Arts Center is on the high school campus. "Hey, Randi? Don't worry about the shoulder sit. We'll figure it out this evening before the show, all right?"

"Okay," Randi says meekly, and the two of them walk out, shouldering their textbook-laden backpacks, to head back to class. Randi's grateful to have a friend like Paige.

"At least the fish dive went well. Other than your fall, I thought it was pretty good. Don't you?" Paige asks.

"I guess," Randi replies. But she has severe doubts about EVER doing that terrifying stunt again. She can't bear the thought of it. No way. They'll have to do something else. Not the shoulder sit. She's absolutely sure of it. Even if Deanne hovers, waiting for the chance to take over. But hopefully, by then, it will be too late for her to do that.

18

CONCERT

Randi

Go for it! Maybe that double (or triple)
pirouette will work out this time.

Randi watches the three musketeers chant backstage in their usual pre-performance ritual, to the amusement of the rest of the cast.
"Pat a cake, pat a cake, dance if you can!
Yes ma'am, yes ma'am, of course we can!
Graceful, flowing, nailing every step!
We can, we can, dance with pep!"
They finish with hoots and high fives. At the moment, she wishes she had that kind of camaraderie with a group instead of being the one alone, who everyone supposedly looks up to and follows. The stress makes her feel trapped in a pressure cooker with no way out.

Lisa, from Intermediate ballet, rolls her eyes. "How annoying. They're so childish."

"I think it's cute," Annie says, passing by. "At least it's something fun and positive for them to do before the show."

Randi tries to focus, but is too distracted by her own pre-performance jitters. When she and Jack arrived before call time to work on that terrifying shoulder sit, she'd flat-out refused to do it. After what happened this morning, she was way too scared. Miss Val finally came up with an alternative, a much easier move Randi felt more confident with. It's a simple stag lift in which Jack turns slowly around, one time, holding her in position. Nothing amazing or earthshattering about it. But this, she can live with. She thinks back to this morning and feels her face flush with embarrassment all over again at the thought of lying on top of Jack, spread-eagled and undignified. *Ugh. No one will ever forget that. That's how everyone at ballet, who I have to face every day, will always think of me.*

Once all the performers are seated on the floor backstage, Miss Val begins her usual pep talk. "Are we all happy and excited tonight?" She smiles and looks around at the sea of faces peering back at her. "I am. Do you know why?" She looks around again. "I'm excited because we have the best cast in the whole wide world. And I've already seen how well you can perform *Giselle*. You guys are the greatest!"

The little ones giggle, and Randi snaps to, previously unaware she'd been staring at Jack the whole time, imagining his arms around her. *What? Pull it together now.*

"Okay then, let's get out there and have fun! All right, time to be extra quiet and get in our places to begin."

The house lights have already flickered on and off, so the patrons in the audience will know it's time to be seated. The villagers scurry to their starting positions. Standing behind the closed front curtains, Randi listens as the narrator begins to tell the audience the story of *Giselle*. He's a dad of a former student who takes his job seriously, graciously returning each year at the chance to announce the story ballet and put his own twist on it. He wears a different hat each time he goes out, usually between acts, and this time he's donning one of the hunter green triangular hats. As always, he's wearing a black suit.

"Tonight," he begins, "The Dance Centre will perform the story ballet, *Giselle*. This poor, young maiden has fallen in love with Albrecht. The prince, who, of course as these fairy tales always go, is already betrothed to another."

Randi hears the audience snicker while her heart pounds fiercely in her chest. *Calm down!* She remembers her Nana is in the audience and how far she's come to watch her perform. *I can't let her down.*

"Of course, our fair maiden is unaware of this and dances incessantly with him. This worries her poor mother, because her beautiful daughter has a weak heart and really shouldn't exert herself so much. But, what can she do? She's tried to warn her daughter, but do you think that works?" The audience laughs again as he continues to engage them.

Randi's own heart feels weak at the moment, and she leans into the wall on stage left as a wave of nauseous panic threatens to bowl her over. She closes her eyes tightly and shakes her head, trying to make the sensation go away. *Come on, Randi. It's probably not as bad as it seems. Just psych yourself out.* She inhales deeply, holds her breath, and then slowly lets it out. *You can do this.* She begins to feel better. *I just have to dance as well as I can and only count on myself. I can do this.* She wonders how that can really work while partnering, but forces herself to breathe in and out again, her heart and mind slowly drifting back to normal. *Good, it's helping.*

Randi feels the side lights warming the stage as Act One unfolds. She smiles at Jack as he takes her hand in the duet. During the fish dive, his hand slips and she hits her knuckles on the floor. It stings, but at least he doesn't drop her. The dance now begins to go more smoothly, but still a little shaky. *Time to focus.* She nails her double *pirouette* into a *penché arabesque* and comes up grinning. They've come back and are in sync. She smiles cautiously, recognizing the shift into becoming one with the ballet. The outside world melts away as the villagers celebrate, the hunters hunt, and the gypsies entertain. The curtains close at the end of Act One and the crew gets to work setting the stage for the next act.

"Oh crap! My zipper's stuck. Ugh. Help!" Willow's friend is in near hysterics.

The older girls huff and puff into the dressing room.

"Chill out, girl!" Brindle says, grabbing the zipper and pulling downward to start over. "There you go. All fixed." Miss Val's oldest daughter is always so matter-of-fact.

"Thank you," she mouths and the hustle and bustle of costume changes escalates around them.

Costume parts lay scattered around Brindle, who's sitting on the floor retying her *pointe* shoe ribbons, while Paige frantically rifles through the makeup artillery littering the counter.

Randi quickly leaves the chaotic dressing room and notices Todd looking half-dead by the doorway. "Are you okay?"

"Not really." He tells her he must've caught the bug from Jack last night.

The stage lights flicker, signaling the cast to get into their places for Act Two. The narrator finishes his spiel, and Miss Val tells them to hurry up.

A young Wili stands onstage crossing her legs and wiggling. "I gotta pee," she says out loud. "But I have this stupid leotard on underneath and it will take too long. Ooh."

Randi knows how that is. Dancers have to learn to use the bathroom without completely disrobing.

"I'm scared," says a little chipmunk. "I want my mommy." Her hood droops adorably into her face.

Miss Val is busy adjusting her son's skunk tail and Randi watches Paige go over to the little girl and lean down.

"I used to be scared, too, but not anymore. I think it's a lot of fun now. There's really nothing to be afraid of. You did such a good job this morning. We'll just do it again. Okay?"

The little girl crinkles her face into a cute little grin and the stage mom off to the side gives her two thumbs up. Paige walks back to her position and Act Two begins.

Beneath their ghostly gowns, the Wilis dance eerily in the darkened lake scene. Randi begins her dreaded *piqué* turn circle trying extra hard to spot, with stage lights disorienting her. One, two, three . . . *Will I make it?* Then she remembers Miss Val's words. "Don't think of that last turn as the end. Picture it as the beginning of the next sequence. And breathe!"

It works, and she finishes the combination with a culminating crescendo! At least that's what the *saut de chat* feels like. The Intermediate class gets down to business and dances poor Hilarion to his death. Those Wilis are on fire! Randi watches, while waltzing in the periphery, and thinks his fever might be adding to how real this looks.

A loud little voice is heard coming from the audience. "Is Sophia a ghost?"

Probably her little brother.

Sophia stifles a laugh when Randi gives her the eye. A wee bird wanders on from the wings and Randi takes a wider than practiced circle to ease the child offstage gracefully.

Randi's mind pulls from the scene as the dreaded lift approaches. But they have taken it out and changed the stunt entirely. *Why am I so scared now?* The lighting and music continue to darken in mood, sending her into a downward spiral. Hues of violet, red, and purple spin around her in dizzying swirls, camouflaging the other dancers. She dances almost on automatic as her thinking, logical mind takes over. *What am I doing? I'm a dancer. It's what I want to be. Playing the lead in Giselle! I've got to be at my best here and make this matter.* Her body continues going through the motions of the dance as she swirls toward Jack. Ducking under his arm, she smells his perspiration. It isn't bad, it just triggers confusing feelings. She shakes her head slightly when she passes behind him, to clear her thoughts.

As if a bolt of lightning strikes her, it becomes crystal clear. *We have to do the shoulder sit! It's what we've practiced for months. I can't let fear overpower me. Right now, I am the prima ballerina!* She waltzes by her partner and looks him in the eye. Somehow, she needs to get his full, thinking attention. *How?* Then she knows. She remembers what that dancer at the wedding in Phoenix had told her. That it's simply a decision to just do it. State of mind. *And it's what Nana's been saying all along, too.*

"Jack!" she whispers. "We're going to do it."

His brow furrows and he looks confused.

Crap! There's only one more phrase before it's time.

She shoots him her most serious look when she slows to face him in the *soutenu* turn and says in a forced whisper, "I'm going to go for the shoulder sit. Be ready!"

He nods, almost imperceptibly, just before she turns around to prepare for the lift. *This is it. Just do it.*

Pushing down into her *soussus*, her toes pulling inward beneath, Randi feels Jack's hands close tightly on her hips. *Good, they're not shaking.* She grasps his wrists in readiness while bending her knees in *plié* just enough for the jump. *Okay. Here we go. You can do it. You're the Dance Centre's prima ballerina!*

Randi uses her legs and feet, the way she's been taught, straightening her knees completely at the end of the jump, pressing through her entire foot, and finishing with pointed toes. She looks straight ahead at the lights in the booth, keeping her arms locked in position. She arches her back and her bottom slides backward to rest on his shoulder, stopping just before going off his back. She can't believe it. *We did it!* She quickly lifts her chin with pride and pulls her arms upward into a graceful arc.

The audience claps wildly as the duo turns a 360, and Randi can't help but smile through tears of joy. She could stay there forever. But she doesn't. Jack pops her off his shoulder and places her in front of him. The rest of the ballet must go on. She takes a deep, grateful breath before stretching downward into a *penché arabesque*. Randi and Jack perform their passionate farewell dance and the curtains close as he's clutching her cross.

The cast scrambles and lines up for the finale. When the curtains reopen, the young villagers go out first, followed by the hunters. When the forest animals venture on from stage right, their line meanders almost drunkenly and they wobble and stare out into the audience, blinded by the bright lights. After bowing, one of them stops, frozen in place, while the others walk backward to allow room for the next group. Much cajoling and pointing from offstage does no good, but the audience loves it. Finally, the little chipmunk is taken back with the Wilis after they curtsy. The applause increases when Randi and Jack lead the cast in one final bow. They've done it, and it feels great! The cast hoots and hollers and then Todd runs forward and cartwheels off the front of the stage just as the curtains close.

The little ones start to run forward, but Miss Val stops them just in time with her loud whistle. She only uses that when she has to. Like now, when chaos erupts. The curtains open again, and she walks forward to address the audience.

"Thank you all for coming and we hope you enjoyed our show." She turns to face the cast and leads the audience in another round of applause. "Good job, you guys!" Then she focuses on Todd coming up the stairs from the audience and points at him. "Except for that last stunt you pulled, young man." Laughter floods the crowd. He sheepishly ducks his head and slides behind the Wilis. "These kids are the greatest, and we've had so much fun." She invites everyone to stay for the reception of cookies and juice and tells them about the last performance of *Giselle* coming up at the San Diego County Fair in a couple weeks. Miss Val proceeds to hand out pink carnations to each of the performers, and the curtains close again.

The younger students are taken to the auditorium so their parents can claim them, and the older ones head to the dressing rooms to change and pack their things.

Miss Val sticks her head in the door of the girl's dressing room. "Great job, guys! Wow, Randi! You really nailed that shoulder sit. It was great!"

"Thanks. It felt good, too." Randi can hardly believe they'd pulled it off. She feels ready to jump out of her skin, she's so excited.

Then Miss Val gives Randi a stern look. "You're lucky it worked out, though, you know? It was risky to just go for it, with no practice. But—" She pauses. "I'm proud of you."

Randi breathes a sigh of relief.

"It *was* really good," Deanne says. "I'm happy for you, Randi. Honest."

Randi smiles. "You were good, too."

"It was fantastic!" Paige croons. "I never had any doubts, though. I knew you could do it." She reaches up to brush a hair from Randi's eyes. "Your locks are glued to your forehead. You better clean up before you go greet your fans."

Annie, the three musketeers, the Intermediate students—they all congratulate her on her wonderful performance. Randi is on cloud nine and feels ready to take on the world, but first she must get more presentable.

Randi grabs a comb and quickly fixes her hair. "Come on, Paige. Our fans are waiting for us."

"I know. I know. Just hold your horses." Paige gathers her makeup items, which are strewn all over the counter in front of the big mirror, and crams them into her purse.

Randi grabs the lipstick. "Wait, can I use this?"

"What for?"

"I just want to put more on. So I can look nice, okay?"

"Knock yourself out, girl. But we're already done performing."

Randi smiles and takes off the cap.

"Oh, I get it," says Paige. "You want to look nice for *him*."

"Don't be silly," Randi says, with a guilty grin, and finishes with the lipstick. "Here you are. Now let's go."

The two make their way across the stage as the backdrop is being lowered. They walk down the steps and out the stage door into the auditorium. The packed place practically pulses with everyone talking excitedly in groups and posing for pictures. Miss Val holds several bouquets of flowers and talks to a group of parents, grandparents, and little performers. She poses with two little forest animals while a dad snaps their picture. "Thanks, Val. We'll see you at the fair," he says.

The videographer comes over and aims his camera at Paige and Randi. "So, how do you think it went?"

"Great!" Randi answers.

"Yes, fantastic," Paige says. "It was awesome, and I can't wait to do it again!"

The man finds another target and wanders away.

"I never know what to say," Randi says. "It makes me uncomfortable."

"Look." Paige elbows her friend and nods toward a group of teenagers. "Isn't that Jack? Who's he with?"

Just then, Jack pulls a tall, slender girl in close and leans his head over to touch hers.

Randi looks on in dismay, fighting back a wave of nausea. She knows she doesn't own him. They aren't boyfriend and girlfriend. She just has a thing for him. And she realizes then what a silly crush it is. But she's still hurt. The former high she'd felt right after the performance quickly dissolves.

"Are you all right?" Paige asks.

Randi turns away and takes a deep breath. "Yeah, I'm fine."

Mom comes over and hugs Randi first and then Paige before handing each of them a bouquet of red roses. "You girls did great."

"Thanks, Mrs. Boles. These are beautiful."

"Yes, they are. Thanks, Mom." Randi breathes in the heady scent and tries to escape the heartache inside. She watches Paige's mom hug her friend tightly and hand her another bunch of flowers.

"I thought you said you weren't going to do the shoulder sit anymore," Mom says.

"I wasn't." She forces a smile. "But I changed my mind."

Nana wraps Randi into a bear hug and practically squeezes the wind out of her.

"Oh, Nana, I did it!"

"Yes, you certainly did, my little coyote. You more than did it. You crushed it." Nana laughs. "Is that how they say it?"

Randi laughs, too. "Close enough. Thank you. I love you."

"I never doubted your abilities for a minute, Randi." The short, stocky woman pulls away and looks at her through tears of pride. "I love you, too."

Dad steps in to give her a hug and congratulates his "prima ballerina" on her wonderful performance.

Even David ventures over, with a couple of his friends, and says he liked the performance. "It was a lot better than I thought it would be."

"David!" Randi exclaims, smacking him lightly with her bouquet.

"Let's go get more cookies," he says, and she and Paige follow him.

Randi tries her best to swallow her feelings and makes small talk with everyone who comes up to congratulate her on her amazing performance. The message begins to sink in. She's done a good job tonight. It actually is pretty spectacular dancing the lead in *Giselle*. *Giselle*, of all ballets! She is the star! She even manages to hide her feelings when Jack and his new girlfriend come over to say hi. He's just a guy. Dancing the lead is so much more important. In spite of this little setback, it has been a fabulous evening. She'll make sure to revel in it forever. She now has a renewed confidence that she can do whatever it is that she sets her mind to. She's on fire!

19

Interim

Randi

Take a break and rejuvenate!

The Dance Centre takes a week off classes and rehearsals to regroup after the busy performance week. The fair is still a couple weeks away and now the students have a chance to catch up on sleep and study for finals at school. Randi appreciates how Miss Val helps them all lead balanced lives without making the kinds of demands on the families' time or budget many studios do.

David usually drives by himself to school these days. Now that Randi has her learner's permit and is trying to get all the practice she can, Mom lets her drive to school and then takes the car to work.

"Watch out for that cone!"

"I know. I know. I see it!" Randi steers around the rolling orange hindrance successfully. "I am getting better, don't you think?"

"Yes, dear, you are. But don't get overly confident. Anything can happen."

Randi's phone chimes, indicating a text, and she glances down.

"Don't you dare!" Mom warns.

"I wasn't going to do anything!"

She pulls into the drop-off lane, and Mom walks around to get into the driver's seat. "Have a good day, honey."

"You too, Mom." Randi walks quickly toward class as the bell rings. She sits down at the desk next to Paige and takes a notebook from her backpack.

The teacher is already going over what to study for the final. "Yes," she says. "*Pride and Prejudice* will definitely be on the test. You should have a decent knowledge of everything we've covered this semester."

Randi groans. She's run out of paper. "Paige, do you have some paper I could borrow?"

Paige opens her binder and hands her a stack of college-ruled paper. "Is this enough?" she whispers.

Randi nods and begins copying notes from the board. It seems like she's writing the entire period. When the bell rings, she shakes out her right hand and puts the completely filled three pages—both sides— into her binder. On to the next class—biology. Almost as much writing there, too. By lunch break, her hand is about ready to fall off, and she's starving.

"What did you bring, Paige?" Randi asks, plopping down next to her, on the tree well in the quad.

Paige opens her baggie and before taking a bite, says, "Tuna fish. How about you?"

"Cold, leftover chicken. Want to trade?"

"No thanks. I'm good."

"Hey, Paige. You gotta see this." Randi pulls her phone from her pocket and flips through the passing images. "I found this really cool cat video game. Wanna see?"

She offers Paige her phone, but only gets the evil eye in return.

"What?"

"School is enough of a game for me. Come on, Randi." Paige glowers at her semi-warningly. She doesn't have much patience for these kinds of "time wasters," as she calls them.

Just then, Randi sees Jack walking across campus holding hands with his new girlfriend. She sighs, but then quickly turns toward her lunch so Paige won't catch on.

"What?" Paige asks.

"Nothing, just my lunch sucks," Randi fibs. *Having a crush on Jack is so embarrassing.*

"Oh, too bad, so sad." Paige wiggles gleefully, exaggerating her culinary enjoyment.

Randi picks at a chicken leg. "I wish finals were over and we could already have our summer. And I can't wait to go to the women's march next January."

"Don't wish your life away, my friend. Life's too short. But I'm looking forward to it, too," Paige says, taking another bite of her sandwich.

"Yeah. I'm glad Miss Val and Brindle are going to the march. And you and me, and our moms."

Just then, Todd and two other guys come over—pushing, pulling, and razzing each other—and eventually sit down with them.

Todd pats his head carefully. "Is my hair okay, Paige?"

"Turn around so I can see."

"Is it all good?"

"Yup, lovely as usual." Paige giggles.

"What are you doing this summer, Randi?" Todd asks.

"Driving a lot, I hope, so I can get my license. But to tell you the truth, being the one in charge of a moving vehicle makes me nervous."

Todd shakes his head and smiles, like he doesn't get it. "And you, Paige. What about you?" He scoots closer to get out of the sun.

"What about me?" Paige asks, giving him a nudge back into the sun.

Todd snorts. "What are you doing this summer?"

"I don't know yet. I haven't really had time to think about it. But I'd like to get my permit. And you, Todd?"

"What about me?" Todd scoffs.

"Oh brother."

Randi laughs. Her friend has such a relaxed way, that she can't help but envy her. Giving it a try, she says to the guy next to her, "You want the rest of my chicken?"

He snatches the container from her. "Sure. Thanks."

"I'm planning to have a great summer," Todd says. "Thank you for asking, Paige. I plan on sleeping late, going to the beach, and working as little as possible."

"How productive of you," Paige responds. "It must be nice to have such lofty goals."

A scantily clad blonde saunters over, followed by a group of her clones.

"Hey. What are you guys doing over here?" their leader asks. "I thought you guys were coming with us." She pushes her long pink bangs behind her ear and looks at them through thick, blackened eyelashes while the other girls giggle.

"Sure. We were just on our way," one of the boys says. He stands up with his buddy and nudges Todd.

"Go ahead, dude," Todd says, turning back to Randi.

One of the other girls whines. "But we have to practice our routine. The dance room is open now."

"I'll be there after lunch. There's enough time in class."

As they leave, Randi smiles as politely as she can, even though she doesn't care for them at all. "What's their problem, anyway?"

"They think they're the dancing queens of the world. Too snooty for me, that's for sure," Paige says, dusting the sandwich crumbs from her lap. "I'm just glad we only have to see them at school and not at the Dance Centre."

"They wouldn't be caught dead at our studio. They think they're too good for us," Randi says. She finishes her banana and walks over to the trash can. When she returns, she looks around before speaking. "I heard their recital was, like, four hours long! Can you believe it?"

Todd frowns. "Where'd you hear that?"

"One of the girls I babysit takes classes there. Her parents said it was a marathon. Their poor kid fell asleep before she even got to go on stage and they had to wake her up. The costume cost $150 and she only got to wear it once."

"How sad," Paige says. "Did you tell the mom about our story ballets?"

"Yeah. Her mom said she might join in the fall, if the girl even wants to dance anymore."

Lunch period ends and the three head for the dance room. A group of girls stand around the water fountain in the studio. Nuevo High School has a dance production class for the most experienced dancers and they receive fine arts credit instead of P.E.

"She thinks she's so cool dancing the lead in some stupid ballet," says a tall, skinny girl, pulling her lavender ponytail forward to examine the split ends.

The short brunette says in a loud whisper, "I know. Who do they think they are, anyway?"

The first girl turns toward Randi. "Did you hear our studio took first place at the competition this weekend?"

"Oh. Congratulations," Randi answers. She and Paige stretch on the floor and can't help but hear their usual snide remarks—and their lack of reciprocal congratulations on the Dance Centre's successful concert.

The group by the fountain continues bantering about so and so being fat and, "No doubt unpopular." And about how cute that guy is and, "Why is he going out with her? She doesn't even have any friends."

Randi can't stand how snarky and unfriendly those girls are, but she does her best to be nice anyway. She reminds herself that it serves no purpose to mimic their behavior and forces herself to rise above her angry feelings. At least, that way, she won't have anything to feel guilty about later. She's glad both she and Paige are trying to put their best foot forward whenever they can. It's still their pact with each other, and besides, it just feels better.

The students are working on their own group choreography, which determines their final grade. The popular girls take dance at that other studio and are very cliquish and exclusive when it comes to including anyone else, except the boys. Randi and Paige are working on a lyrical piece that includes a little hip hop mixed in. Jack makes a brief appearance and jumps into a back tuck between moves.

"Hey, Jack! Could you do one of those in our dance, too?" the blonde calls from the other side of the room.

Those girls make Randi sick. *They are so shallow.*

He agrees to make a quick pass across with a roundoff followed by a back tuck.

They all hoot and flirt until the teacher calls them back to order. "You have to show your dances in two days. Now, get back to work and stop goofing around!"

The popular girls keep hogging the sound system to practice their dance; they stop and start their music at least a dozen times before the teacher finally catches on and lets another group use it.

Paige walks up, plugs in her iPod, and bounces to the beat. She's almost always in a good mood and Randi hopes that more of her friend's positive attitude will rub off on her. Some, she's noticed, already has. They begin their dance in a Martha Graham-type contraction—the right arm curves upward, a contemporary twist, signifying a change in emotion.

After school, David takes off with his friends, so Randi calls her mom to come get her and Paige. There's a new frozen yogurt place in town that just opened, and the Advanced ballet group is going to meet there, except for Annie. She already had plans.

Randi and Paige arrive early and order different things. That way, they can sample each other's selections and get a better idea about what to order next time, *if* they decide it's good enough to come back. Paige gets chocolate, swimming in a strawberry glaze.

"Mm. That looks good. Is it?" Randi's mouth waters just looking at it.

"I don't know yet. Give me a minute, will ya?" Paige cracks a smile and sits at one of the larger tables.

The chimes in the door tinkle when the three musketeers come in. They wave and head straight to the counter. The bells chime again and Todd makes his entrance and walks directly to the table. He pulls out a chair next to Randi, turning it backward before sitting down. The baseball cap on his head is also backward.

"Hello, ladies. And how are we doing?"

"Well, Randi's just peachy. Can you tell?" Paige points at her peach-covered vanilla frozen yogurt.

Todd laughs. "That's awesome. And I, of course, am awesome, too. Thanks for asking."

Randi gives him a sidelong glance, wondering why he has to be so goofy all the time. "Where's Jack?"

"Oh, he had to work. Or something. He told me, but I can't remember." Todd pushes up from his chair. "So, what's good here? What should I get?"

"The choice is all yours, my friend." Paige shakes her head at him and laughs.

The three younger girls join them as Todd goes over to order.

Paige swipes a spoonful from Randi's bowl. "Not bad. What do *you* think?"

"It's okay, but I like yours better."

The girls talk about the concert and how well it went and complain about their upcoming finals in school.

"I have *so* much studying to do. I'm worried about biology the most," Randi says. *I'm on my own for studying since Paige is taking chemistry and needs time to prepare for that.*

Todd returns with a huge banana split-looking thing. "You'll do fine, Randi. I think you're really smart." He pauses to take a big bite. "A lot smarter than me, anyway."

Randi laughs nervously. "No. I don't think so. English and math are hard for me, too."

"Well, just sayin'." He scoots closer and grins.

Deanne pushes her bowl away. "I'm stuffed. I think *I'm* ready for finals."

"Really?" Randi says, glancing at Paige.

Paige stares back, then says, "Good for you, Deanne."

The chatter in the shop increases in volume, making their conversation more difficult to follow. The Yogurt Cave is a bright, cheery place with lots of after-school traffic. Pop tunes play in the background and Randi thinks she'll definitely want to come back. *After* finals are over, that is.

20

THE FAIR PERFORMANCE

Deanne

*Go home—close the door, put on your
favorite music, and dance your heart out!*

Deanne and her mother work their way through the crowds on the midway—past shouting vendors, roaring roller coasters, and clanging bells signifying prizes won. After parking in the performers' lot, they always take this route to get to the Showcase Stage where they perform. A large billboard advertises the summer lineup for the Grandstand Stage. Most are tribute bands, but a few are bigger name groups.

"What time is it, Mother?" Deanne shouts above the crowd. She is eyeing a poster displaying a huge deep-fried, chocolate-covered Twinkie. "Do you think we have time for one of those?"

Mother laughs. "Not before your performance, you don't. I don't think it would be that great of an idea afterward, either, for that matter."

"I was just joking. I'm too nervous anyway."

"Oh, darling, you'll do fine." Mother's voice is barely audible over the noise, but she can make out the words from watching her lips.

Deanne adjusts the costume bag over her shoulder. "I just want to make it to the stage and get ready. I can relax and have fun later."

Miss Val is already there when they arrive, talking to the stage manager and unpacking boxes of props and accessories. Brindle runs over, takes Deanne's costumes, and leads her to the dressing tent behind the stage. It's loud here, too, but at least you can hear each other speak.

Sophia opens the flap and dumps her pile onto the floor in the corner. "Let's all do rides together after, okay?" She ties her shiny, black hair into a ponytail and kicks her ballet bag across the floor toward them.

"Oh no! I think I forgot my ballet slippers!" Deanne shrieks, frantically searching through her bag.

"Didn't your mom remind us to bring our soft shoes at the last rehearsal?" Sophia asks.

"Yes," Brindle answers. "She doesn't want us in toe shoes. She always brings plenty of rosin, but no amount is really enough here."

Deanne stands up after unsuccessfully rifling through her things. "Crap! What am I going to do?" She can't just have stocking feet. The surface on this stage makes you feel like you're skating on ice. It's that slippery.

Brindle looks up at her. "Go ask my mom. She usually brings a few extras in the prop box."

Deanne dashes out of the tent and runs around to the stage where Miss Val and her husband are laying out the tumbling mats. Her teacher is wearing a big, floppy garden hat and is kneeling down, taping the ends of the mats together.

"Miss Val," Deanne pants. "I forgot my ballet slippers!"

"Hmm." Miss Val stares up at her. After a long pause, she finally says, "Look in that box over there. I put a few pairs in before the concert. They might still be there."

Deanne turns without delay and runs over to the pile of accessories. She compares the two pairs she finds, chooses the bigger ones, and heads back to the dressing tent.

Miss Val calls after her. "Make sure you put them back right after the performance!"

"I will. Thanks!" *How could I have forgotten shoes, of all things?*

By the time everyone is warmed up and in their places, a gentle wind kicks up. Deanne repeatedly pulls down her peasant skirt to keep it where it belongs. She notices she isn't the only one. Oh well, at least the breeze is keeping it from being so hot.

Randi makes a sour face when Jack and his girlfriend act all lovey-dovey over on the bleachers next to the stage. Performing here at the county fair means they don't have access to side wings and curtains. Everything is visible, including Randi's apparent jealousy. Deanne enjoys watching the little side show, assured that no one will notice her interest in it.

When the music begins, the cast transforms into the village scene. Giselle dances with her mother and friends. Then she dances with her new beau, Albrecht. She beams radiantly, gracefully gliding through her role. They are very much in love; but later, as his engagement to another is revealed to her, she'll die of a broken heart.

In Act Two, Deanne feels her shoe slipping off. *Crap.* She wishes she was wearing her own slippers. She'd sewn her elastics close to the center, in back, to prevent this from happening with her narrow heels. She senses them sliding farther down. *Perhaps I'll glide along the floor and not jump very high.* The next combination has three *tour jetés*. That's when one shoe goes flying. She finds herself spotting it, the moving slipper, instead of a fixed object, and watches a guy in the audience catch it. *How embarrassing.* Moving on, like a good seasoned dancer, she tries not to show it in her face. Randi glares disapprovingly at her when she passes and looks a little out of sorts. *Probably still jealous.* Now, the other slipper is barely dangling on her foot, so she rakes it off on the huge speaker on stage right as she circles by. At least her legs feel even again, but now she has to be extra careful in her stocking feet. Luckily, her toes are sweaty and actually stick a little better than with the shoes on.

Finally, the ending scene finishes, with Jack clinging to Giselle's cross. Deanne steps over a hunter's fallen hat lying on the stage floor and makes her way over to her finale line. *Is that Bree in the audience? What is she holding?* After all the bowing and applauding, Miss Val comes out and begins another round of applause for the cast and thanks everyone for coming.

The crowd quickly disperses and Deanne sees Randi talking with Todd, Paige, and Brindle. She hurries over to be included.

"Hey, Deanne," Brindle says. "They invited us to hang out with them and go on rides together. Would that be okay with your mom?"

"I'll ask. I'm sure it would be." Deanne sincerely hopes so. It isn't every day they get an invitation to hang out with the big kids. It's what she's been praying for.

Deanne turns from Brindle when she hears Randi oohing and aahing. Bree stands slightly away from the group, smiling tentatively. It actually *is* her.

"Is this your baby, Bree?" Paige asks. "What a cutie."

Bree is holding a little pink bundle in her arms. "Yes. This is Lily." She looks sheepishly up at the group.

Randi strokes a little foot poking out of the blanket. "She's beautiful. How old is she?"

Bree seems to loosen up a little. "One month old today." She rocks the infant back and forth. "You guys did great. I didn't even know you were performing down here today. And Randi, wow!" She stops for a moment. "You've sure come a long way. I'm impressed."

"Well," Randi says, "I'm nowhere near as good as you."

That's an understatement. Deanne looks at the stroller behind Bree and the piles of stuff in it. "We miss you. Are you coming back to ballet?" She feels sorry for the poor girl. *Probably no more dance in her future.*

Bree laughs nervously before answering. "Oh, I don't know. Probably not. I kind of have my hands full these days." She leans down and kisses the baby's forehead.

Miss Val walks into the group and hugs Bree. "You know you're welcome back anytime. Randi had some awfully big shoes to fill, but I think she did a pretty good job, don't you think?"

"Definitely," Bree says, turning her focus toward Deanne. "And speaking of shoes—"

Everyone laughs.

Deanne gasps and looks around frantically for the guy who caught her shoe.

"Don't worry," Miss Val says. "He returned it after the performance. And as for you, young lady, perhaps you'll plan better next time?"

They all laugh again and say goodbye to Bree before getting on to the task of deciding who's going where with whom. Hanging out? Carnival rides? Eating junk food? Deanne convinces Mother to let her join them and is allowed to go for two hours. It will be the eight of them: her, Brindle, Sophia, Randi, Paige, Todd, and even Jack and his girlfriend, Marie.

"Let's go change and get ready," Sophia says, "before the lines for the rides get too long."

"It's not like Disneyland," Paige says. "The place just gets more fun." She picks up one of the Wili weeds and hands it to Miss Val.

"Thank you, Paige. If you guys want to put your things in that big box over there, we'll take them out on the cart with all the costumes and other stuff. You can come to the studio next week for them." Miss Val points to JP, who's sitting on the stack of tumbling mats checking in everyone's rental costumes.

"That would be awesome," Todd says, reaching over to pick out some straw from Randi's hair, which had blown in on the breeze.

"Thanks," Randi says, "to both of you." She giggles nervously. "To Miss Val for taking our stuff and to you for getting the hay out of my hair."

They make their way to the changing tents and hurry to clear the area for the next group coming in to perform. Deanne has already returned her other shoe and quickly changes and packs her things.

Brindle brushes her long blonde hair and scoops it back into a ponytail. "Ready?"

Annie pokes her head in through the tent flap. "You guys have a good summer, okay?"

"You too," Sophia says. "Hey, how come you're not going to go for rides and eat junk food with us?"

"Hah! You know me and food. Let's just say we have an interesting relationship. Anyway, I have a modeling shoot tonight and I have to get ready for that." The room darkens again and she's gone.

"What's with her, anyway? We all know she could stand a little more padding on those skinny bones of hers," Brindle says.

"She just doesn't eat much. That's all," Deanne says. "I don't think she's anorexic or anything."

The three musketeers gather their bags and push out through the tent flap, smiling at the heavily made-up girls coming in. Deanne figures they'll be performing a bunch of unrelated dances to loud hip hop music, shaking their booties and wearing seductive costumes. Her parents wouldn't let her be caught dead in such things. That's for sure.

"This is so much fun, you guys. We get to hang out unsupervised." Sophia's little body practically quivers with excitement.

"It is, huh?" Deanne walks between her two friends, wrapping both her arms around their shoulders, prompting them to skip to catch up with the others. The midway is even louder than when she passed through it earlier with her mother.

"Hey, pal. Win this giant panda for your girlfriend!" shouts one of the vendors. "All ya gotta do is make three baskets out of five! Isn't she worth it?"

Deanne watches Randi's cheeks flush pink as Todd shakes his head at the guy. *Poor Todd. He probably kind of likes Randi, but she only has eyes for Jack.* Just then, Jack pulls Marie over to the booth and hands the man a ticket.

"One shot, in! Two shots, in! Third—and fourth—missed."

He groans.

"Come on now, Jack. You can do it," encourages Paige.

"Fifth shot, in!" the man yells.

The group cheers; Jack hands Marie a huge, overstuffed bear; and she beams up at him.

Next stop is the giant Ferris wheel. Deanne looks forward to getting an expansive view over the entire fairgrounds. Jack and Marie get into the first bucket and then Todd gets into the second, pulling Randi in with him. *Interesting.*

Paige smirks at Randi and raises her eyebrows. "Come on, Deanne. Come with me?"

Deanne says, "Sure," and climbs into the swaying seat. They ride partway up before the big machine jolts to a stop to let in Brindle and Sophia.

"I think we danced pretty well today, don't you?" Paige asks, leaning over Deanne and looking down her side of the cart.

"Yeah, except for my whole shoe fiasco." Deanne snorts. "That was a little embarrassing."

Paige giggles and Deanne turns to face her.

"I really like Miss Val's *dancespiration,* don't you?"

Deanne thinks about it and smiles. "I actually do that, you know? I go in my room sometimes and turn up the music and dance around. When no one's looking, of course."

"Uh huh. Me too. It's great therapy—especially if I'm having a bad day."

"Ha! It does help, huh?"

"Hey," Paige says, interrupting. "Isn't that Bree?"

Deanne scans the area below, but doesn't see anyone she knows. "Where?"

"Down there." Paige points over Deanne's shoulder. "Over by that fried zucchini place."

Deanne squints and peers down at the crowd below. "Oh yeah. Over there. It is her."

The two sit quietly, watching Bree push the stroller, walking next to her mother.

"I sort of feel sorry for her, don't you?"

"Yes and no, I guess," Paige says, still leaning over Deanne. "Kind of. I think it must have been hard for her to come talk to us like she did. But we all accepted her, didn't we?"

"Of course we did." Deanne agrees. *What choice did we have?* "We couldn't be rude."

"No, I think it's more than that. We all want the best for her. And she is taking responsibility for that baby. She clearly loves her. Don't you think?"

"Mm hmm. But she'll probably never dance again."

"Oh, I don't know about that," Paige says, straightening up, but still looking down at Bree. "I think if it's important enough to her, she'll find a way. Besides, lots of people don't even start dancing until they're grownups. Like Martha Graham, for instance."

"Yeah." Deanne mulls the idea over in her head. "She does seem happy, doesn't she?"

Paige smiles. "In a way, she's kind of lucky, I guess. I've heard sometimes how older women wish they could have kids, but by the time they get around to it their biological clock has run out. That's what happened to my aunt. She thinks it might have been better if she'd accidentally gotten pregnant when she was younger, and had the whole decision taken out of the picture."

"Wow. I never thought about it like that." Deanne finds herself looking down at the former ballerina with new eyes. Maybe it isn't really as bad as it seems. Of course, she'd hate it if it happened to her. But, it never will happen to her. Her strong morals will keep her safe. But on the other hand, it gets her to thinking. She runs her fingers around the smooth surface of her purity ring and thinks back to the agreement she made with her father. *I promise to stay pure for my husband.* After mouthing the words, a blanket of security seems to wrap around her.

But the subject isn't quite as black and white as she once believed it was. Paige is pretty broad-minded about all this, and Deanne is actually a little envious of how grownup she seems. However, Bree hadn't made the wisest choices, obviously. The Ferris wheel begins to turn again and they lose sight of her. The ride turns over and over, and Deanne feels the wind lift the hair up off her neck.

"Nice view, huh?" Paige is smiling and looking across at the racetrack.

Deanne sees the entire infield, including the photo exhibit tent and the little kid rides. "You know, I'm not going to be able to take summer dance classes. I have to go to a church camp up in LA this summer."

"That sounds like fun," Paige says. "How long is it for?"

"Three weeks. But it's right in the middle of summer session," Deanne says wistfully. "I wish I could just stay here and dance with you guys." She's finally become part of the older group and now worries she'll have to start all over again in the fall.

"Oh, you'll have fun. It'll be a different adventure and then you'll join us again in September. Most of us don't attend the whole session, anyway. We all have at least a few conflicts. Besides, Miss Val encourages us to do other things, too. Not just dance."

"I know. I'll just miss everyone."

The wheel turns more slowly and stops periodically to let people off. When it pauses for them to exit their bucket, it occurs to Deanne that they're each walking into their own diverging summer adventures. They're separating from their tightknit dancing family, never to return exactly the same again. It's bittersweet. School and homework loads are over and they'll have a respite from studying. Sure, there will be another performance season, and a different story ballet. But the whole dynamic will change. Deanne hopes that it will be good, too, and she's curious what it might be like next time. As night begins to close around them, the flashing, neon signs brighten the midway and everyone says their goodbyes.

"See you in September!" Jack waves over his shoulder as he and Marie start to walk away, arm in arm.

"Yeah. See ya!" Todd yells back.

"Wait!" Deanne shouts.

They all stop and look at her.

"We should have a party, or something, this summer. Don't you think?" She hopes someone will agree with her. Deanne can't stand the thought of not seeing them all again for that long. Even Randi.

Todd inches closer to Randi, and a grin lights up his face as he casually drapes his arm over her shoulder. "That's a great idea!"

"Oh, I know," Randi says, leaning away from him. "How about a beach party?"

Paige, Brindle, and Sophia all yell, "Yes!" at the same time.

"Text me the info," Jack says, waving again as he turns away with Marie.

They have each other's numbers and Paige takes the lead to arrange it. "Most likely in August," she says.

Oh good. Now Deanne has something to look forward to this summer. *Ooh, and perhaps Randi does, too. She and Todd do look kind of cute together.*

Todd pulls Randi away and bounces along in his gangly gait, with Paige tagging along. The three musketeers meet up with their parents and make their way through the crowds to the parking lot, where they'll each drive home separately. Deanne smiles at her mother when she hands her a little white bag. She opens it carefully then squeals with delight. Inside, wrapped in wax paper, drips a greasy, chocolate-covered, deep-fried Twinkie!

"Thank you, Mother. You're the best."

On the ride back home, Deanne feels satisfied, although a bit bloated from the Twinkie. She knows she's a lucky girl, having two parents who love her. She thinks of Bree's baby, who is growing up with a single mom. And then she considers Paige, who also has a single mother, and Paige's profound way of looking at things. She stares out the window and watches the cars go by on the freeway. Everybody's going somewhere. All following their own destinies, she supposes. What will hers be? Or is there no such thing as destiny? She'll probably never really know. And perhaps that's okay, not knowing. She's beginning to see life more and more as an adventure unfolding, and she decides, at least for the time being, anyway, that she'll just let it.

ABOUT THE AUTHOR

Chi Varnado lives in the backcountry of San Diego County with her husband and a menagerie of animals. She taught dance for thirty-seven years and her own studio staged a story ballet each year—similar to the one in *The Dance Centre Presents Giselle*. This novel is Miss Chi's third published book, written as the first in the upcoming series, *The Dance Centre Presents*. Visit us at DanceCentrePresents.com.

Acknowledgements

Any work of this type requires a village. That is to say, that without the help of everyone involved, this book would not have come to fruition. My dear friends who provided editing, ideas, and support include Susan Nelson, Tammy Greenwood, Bo Varnado, Cindy Zamora, Helen Buchanan, Annette Williams, and numerous other friends and ballerinas. For the business of getting this book published and marketed I'd like to thank Monkey C Media, Susan Farese, Edwin Steen and Guy Buchanan. A special appreciation goes to Pamela Wilder for providing the wonderful cover art. And to my children: Jessie, Kali, and Chance. There are also numerous other kind souls, too many to list here, who have helped bring this project to completion—you know who you are. And last, but not least, to my husband, Kent, for his ongoing belief in my abilities as a writer.

The Beach Party

Brindle

To live is to dance.

Brindle senses the strong current forming behind her. Quickly, she kicks her legs. The momentum of the wave is building. Her heart beats faster and she grabs the boogie board, white-knuckling it, and scoots her weight farther back when the front edge dips. It's a good one.

And then her legs pull back—then downward. The pressure in her chest increases and suddenly there's no air. She holds her breath as the force of the wave above pushes her body down farther. Pinned on the ocean floor, hard shells and seaweed poke into the soft skin of her belly. She presses as hard as she can, with all her might, trying to do a push-up. It's not working.

OTHER BOOKS BY CHI VARNADO

Miss Chi's books are available on Amazon and where all books are sold.

The Tale of Broken Tail

A CANYON TRILOGY
Life Before, During and After
the Cedar Fire
Chi Varnado
"Chi shows us, in this poignant and inspiring story, that there
are things we can never lose. They are our memories and
our stories, and they make us who we are. I met Chi while
writing about the losses along Mussey Grade Road for The
San Diego Union-Tribune." —Elizabeth Fitzsimons